5/97

On the Wings of Peace

On the Wings of Peace

Tom Feelings

CLARION BOOKS ◦ New York

Clarion Books
a Houghton Mifflin Company imprint
215 Park Avenue South, New York, NY 10003
Compilation copyright © 1995 by Sheila Hamanaka
See page 144 for copyright information on individual contributions.

The text is set in 13/18-point Goudy.

For information about permission to reproduce selections from this book,
write to Permissions, Houghton Mifflin Company,
215 Park Avenue South, New York, NY 10003.

Printed in Mexico.

On the wings of peace : in memory of Hiroshima and Nagasaki /
introduction by Sheila Hamanaka.
p. cm.
Compiler: Sheila Hamanaka. Cf. Data sheet.
Summary: Famous authors and illustrators present a collection of prose
and poetry exploring aspects of peace, from issues of personal and community violence
to international conflict, the bombing of Hiroshima and Nagasaki,
and the environmental dangers of nuclear proliferation.
ISBN 0-395-72619-0
1. Peace—Literary collections. 2. Children's literature.
[1. Peace—Literary collections.] I. Hamanaka, Sheila.
PZ5.057 1995   95-17241
                                                 CIP
                                                 AC
RDT 10 9 8 7 6 5 4 3 2 1

ᔇ Contents

On the Wings of Peace

George Littlechild

✑ Introduction

By Sheila Hamanaka

August 6, 1945: During a war that engulfed most of the world, human beings created and used a secret weapon that destroyed a whole city in a single blow. In this city of 350,000 were people like you and me, and they were already suffering from the effects of war—the death of loved ones, starvation, separation. Some of the people in Hiroshima felt totally loyal to their country, some disagreed with the militarists who ran it, some just hated war, many were too young to hate at all. But in a matter of seconds, over half of them were dead or injured. Three days later, a second Japanese city, Nagasaki, was destroyed the same way.

With these bombings a terrible new vision was born—the specter of a time when human beings would be divided into huge gangs that would start to build and hoard the powerful new weapons called atomic bombs. Soon there would be so many weapons that the gangs, either by accident or by design, would be able to destroy the entire world many times over and over again. The vision that seemed only a possibility in 1945 came true. The gangs are called nations and the time is now.

But something else comes out of war: the desire for peace. That is why sixty writers and artists have created this book. Peace, like war, comes out of a vision. To secure peace, the vision must not be of only one person, or two. It will take a lot of us to make peace a reality. It took 160,000 people working night and day for several years to create the atomic bomb. The standing armies of the world today have forces that number in the millions. There are tens of thousands of atomic bombs.

If you think that building peace will be a hard job and take lots of work, night and day, you are right. But the people who are reading this book are special. Most of them are children, and children have very special gifts: the gifts of love and hope and the desire to play with everyone, no matter what color or nationality or religion they are. And that is what peace is all about. Adults, if they care about children, will make it their business to make sure peace happens now and happens everywhere—from family living rooms, to the streets, and to international borders. Adults who give the gift of life to children must make sure that the world is a safe place to grow up and give life to the next generation.

One of the twentieth-century children who inspired the world with her courage was a little girl named Sadako Sasaki. Sadako was almost two years old when the bomb was dropped on her hometown of Hiroshima. Ten years later she developed leukemia, caused by radiation from the atomic bomb. Sadako believed that if she folded a thousand paper cranes she would be granted her wish for life. She folded over a thousand cranes, despite her pain and suffering. After she died, her classmates helped raise a monument in her honor.

This book is our way of folding a thousand paper cranes. If we had asked all the writers and artists and children who believed in peace to contribute we could have filled all the libraries in the world. What you are holding is the work of just a few friends. There are millions of people out there who are flying, now, on the wings of peace. Please join us. The world looks good from up here.

Kam Mak

Nuclear Dawn by Marshall Arisman

ᔑ World War II in the Pacific

by Greg Mitchell

Pearl Harbor and Hiroshima: the two names will be linked forever, signifying the beginning of World War II in the Pacific and its end. Many people today know little of the war in the Pacific beyond those two names. But that conflict did not actually begin with Pearl Harbor and, many believe, it did not require dropping the atomic bomb on Hiroshima for it to end.

The Pacific war had its roots in the 1920s, when militarists gained influence in Japan. The war did not begin, however, until September 18, 1931, when a Japanese general moved his army into Manchuria and installed a puppet leader. The League of Nations (the predecessor of the United Nations) condemned the action. Soon the militarists had assassinated the Japanese premier and seized power. They made plans to invade China, as a first step in gaining control of all East Asia and the Western Pacific—from India to the Philippines.

Japan was motivated by several factors. Colonial powers—particularly England, France, and the Netherlands—had long dominated most of the countries in the region. Now Japan announced its determination to free these colonies and form what it called the Greater Japanese East Asia Co-Prosperity Sphere. What the Japanese militarists were most interested in, however, was gaining access to badly needed oil and raw materials in the area.

With Manchuria and Korea already under its command, Japan inaugurated war with China in July 1937. In this campaign, Japan bombed Chinese cities and killed perhaps as many as 200,000 civilians in what became known as the Rape of Nanking.

The United States responded with strict trade sanctions against Japan. In July 1941, President Roosevelt issued an executive order freezing all Japanese financial assets, and England followed suit. Among other things, these moves would cut off Japan's source of imports such as rubber, scrap iron, and fuel oil.

Japan suffered severely under the embargo, but refused to relinquish its conquests. Instead, it prepared for wider war. Those plans reached a climax on December 7, 1941, with the surprise aerial attack on the U.S. naval base at Pearl Harbor, Hawaii, which killed more than two thousand Americans and devastated the Pacific fleet.

President Roosevelt, calling it a "day that shall live in infamy," asked Congress to declare war on Japan (and, a few days later, on Japan's allies, Germany and Italy). Now the Pacific War, as Americans would come to know it, had begun.

At first the Japanese advanced quickly, overrunning opponents throughout East Asia and the Pacific islands. By late 1942, however, the United States had rebounded from Pearl Harbor. It threw much of its military and industrial might at the Japanese. One American-led triumph followed another: Midway, the Philippines, Iwo Jima, Okinawa.

By the summer of 1945, Japan was surrounded and near collapse. Its supplies of oil and raw materials were virtually halted by a submarine blockade. Its air defenses seemed powerless to prevent U.S. bombers from setting most of its cities aflame. On a single night, firebombings destroyed one-quarter of Tokyo, killing as many as 100,000 civilians.

It was at this point that the atomic bomb came into play.

ɔ

American (along with British) scientists in Los Alamos, New Mexico, and several other sites had secretly attempted to build an atomic bomb for years. Originally, the scientists were told that they were in a race with Germany to create the weapon that could win the war. But as the date approached for testing the device—the summer of 1945—Germany surrendered. This left only Japan (which had never seriously attempted to build the bomb) yet to be defeated.

U.S. planners selected several Japanese cities as likely targets. Although each had some military value to the enemy, the prime purpose of the attack was to display the power of the bomb and "shock" the Japanese into surrender. Therefore, the bomb would be dropped over the center of a city which had not been damaged by earlier bombings, for maximum effect. The planners knew this would likely kill thousands of civilians.

Franklin Roosevelt died in April 1945. This left Harry S. Truman with the responsibility to use—or decline to use—what the new President called "the most terrible thing ever discovered."

The United States, meanwhile, made plans for a massive land invasion of Japan to begin on November 1, 1945—if the war was not over by then. In mid-July, however, the atomic bomb was tested successfully in New Mexico. Several days later, the Allies warned the Japanese that they faced certain ruin if they did not surrender immediately and "unconditionally." However, they did not reveal the existence of the top-secret atomic bomb. The Japanese rejected the ultimatum.

Several days later, on August 6, 1945, an American B-29 bomber, piloted by Paul Tibbets, dropped a single atomic weapon (made with uranium) over Hiroshima, a city of 345,000. It destroyed 60 percent of the city and killed outright at least 100,000 of its residents.

Among the dead were at least a dozen American prisoners of war and several hundred Japanese-Americans who had been visiting the city at the outbreak of war in 1941 (and then were trapped there). The bomb also killed more than ten thousand Koreans who had been forced to work in Japan.

Japanese leaders met to discuss how to respond. There was another shocking development: the Soviet Union, a longtime and hated enemy, had finally declared war on Japan and was marching into Manchuria. Many of the Japanese leaders felt *that* was just as frightening as the atomic bomb.

While the militarists and the peace faction in the Japanese government debated whether to surrender, another U.S. plane dropped a second atomic bomb (this one made with plutonium) over Nagasaki. As expected, it exploded with even greater force than the Hiroshima bomb, but somewhat off target. The death toll was smaller, in the range of 75,000. As in Hiroshima, thousands more would die in the days and months ahead from effects of radiation disease.

There was no "decision," as such, by President Truman to use the second bomb. Before Hiroshima, he had simply ordered that the first two bombs be used as quickly as possible.

Emperor Hirohito threw his support to the peace faction, and on August 14, 1945, announced that Japan would surrender. Truman accepted and called the surrender "unconditional." But actually the United States did allow one major concession. The Emperor would not be jailed or tried as a war criminal (as most Americans demanded). Instead, he would remain on his throne. This was meant to unify the Japanese and allow the United States to demilitarize the country more completely.

Japan formally surrendered in September on board the U.S.S. *Missouri* in Tokyo Bay. The war was over, but the debate over the atomic bombings had just begun.

~

From the beginning, American officials described the use of the atomic bomb against Japan as inevitable. The bomb, in this view, was the only thing that could make the Japanese surrender and prevent the dreaded invasion.

At first, President Truman downplayed the death of Japanese civilians. He referred to Hiroshima as a "military base," and Nagasaki as a center of war industries. Then, when the civilian death toll could not be denied, he justified the bombing on moral grounds by suggesting that up to a million Americans— and many more Japanese—would have perished in an invasion. If this were true, the atomic bombs had saved more lives than they took. Others pointed out that the atomic bombings killed only a few more civilians than the fire-bombing of Tokyo. It was *war* that was bad, not the *weapons of war*.

Some writers and religious leaders condemned the atomic attacks on moral grounds. But, understandably, most Americans, overjoyed at the end of a long and bloody war, accepted them as necessary to produce that victory.

What they did not know—and what many today still do not know—was that by August 1945 victory was certain, even without use of the bomb, and President Truman knew it. The planned invasion almost certainly would not have been necessary to end the war.

This view, surprisingly, was held by many (perhaps most) of America's top military leaders. Years later, General Dwight D. Eisenhower wrote, referring to the atomic attacks on Japan: "It wasn't necessary to hit them with that awful thing." He explained that "Japan was already defeated" and "was, at that very moment, seeking some way to surrender with a minimum loss of 'face.'"

Indeed, we now know, with the release of secret U.S. documents, that the

Japanese were exploring surrender in the weeks before Hiroshima. In his private diary, Truman even referred on July 18, 1945, to a "telegram from Jap emperor asking for peace."

No one will ever know for certain how serious the Japanese were and whether surrender could have been quickly achieved—because the United States chose to use the bomb rather than pursue negotiations.

It is, however, known that many American leaders believed that the *only* point Japan might have insisted on in such talks was the survival of their Emperor and the imperial throne. The United States rejected this idea because it meant that such a surrender would not be "unconditional." Yet, after using the bomb, the United States *accepted* this very condition.

Adding to the likelihood of a rapid surrender was the Soviet Union's attack on the Japanese two days after Hiroshima. Most Americans believed the Soviets were merely trying to "get in on the spoils." In fact, the United States had long urged the Russians to join the conflict. The Soviet entry had always been scheduled for August 1945.

President Truman recognized the significance of the Russian entry in advance. He wrote in his diary on July 17, 1945, that he expected the Soviet entry alone (quite apart from the bomb) to finish off the Japanese. This has led many scholars to suggest that one reason the United States was in such a hurry to use the bomb was because it wanted to hasten the end of the war before the Soviets could claim much Japanese territory.

Surely, critics of the bombing argue, the horror of using the bomb outweighed the risk of seeking a negotiated surrender. When Hiroshima and Nagasaki were destroyed, the planned U.S. invasion of Japan was still nearly three months off.

Another view holds that, all other arguments aside, it was simply inhumane to use such a weapon against innocent civilians. Admiral William Leahy, top military adviser to President Truman in 1945, called the atomic bomb a "barbarous weapon . . . a poisonous thing. . . . My own feeling was that in being the first to use it, we had adopted an ethical standard common to the barbarians of the Dark Ages."

Fifty years after the atomic bombings, controversy continues to swirl around the subject. Much new information about the decision to use the bomb has emerged. Yet many Americans continue to feel that the bombings saved many more lives than they destroyed, and so were justified.

Therefore, the words of Admiral Leahy have as much relevance today as they ever did. "I was not taught to make war in that fashion," he wrote, referring to the atomic attacks, "and wars cannot be won by destroying women and children."

Shinya Fukatsu

ᴗ Floating Lanterns XII

Written and illustrated by Iri and Toshi Maruki
Translated from the Japanese by Nancy Hunter
  with Yasuo Ishikawa

On August sixth every year
    the seven rivers of Hiroshima
    are filled with lanterns
Painted with the names of
    fathers, mothers, and sisters
    they float on their way to the sea

Almost there, pushed back
    flame snuffed out
Darkly coming back in pieces
Tossed by ocean waves

That time, years past
    these same rivers were filled
With the corpses of those
    fathers, mothers, and sisters

T. J. Reddy

A Prayer for Safety

by Nikki Grimes

I shiver in the hall again
while bullets scream by too fast to count,
and no amount of calling me a chicken
will make me dare to go out through that door.

Lord, please make the shooting end.
My friends say prayer won't stop no bullet.
My mother says that may be true,
but that You sure can take away my fear.

I hope she's right,
'cause sometimes I can't sleep at night
not with guns blasting right outside.
I'd hide under the bed if I could move.

Speaking of which,
it would be perfectly okay with me
if we went somewhere else to live.
I'd give almost anything if we could.

In the meantime, God,
please protect my father and my mother,
and keep my little brother safe.
And dear Lord, please take care of me.

Amen. And thanks for listening.

Little Boy and Fat Man photograph by Robert Del Tredici

ᕩ Thoughts from a Nuclear Physicist

by Michio Kaku

I am a nuclear physicist. Sadly, some of my friends design the hydrogen bombs which may eventually end all life on earth.

I made the decision to become a physicist when I was a child of eight, when I heard a story that would change my life. My teacher told the class that a great scientist had just died, perhaps the greatest scientist of our time. She also said that there was a tragic quality, a great sadness, to the story of his life.

Puzzled, I wanted to find out all I could about this man, Albert Einstein, and his theories and his profound regrets. Later, I would finally understand his story. I learned that his theory unlocked the secret of the sun and the stars, but that it also made possible the development of the atomic bomb and with it the power to destroy all life on earth. Einstein once said that if he had known that his work would lead to the atomic bomb, he would have become a fisherman, rather than a physicist. This is because his famous equation, $E=mc^2$, explains not only the nuclear furnace that lights up the stars; it also may someday be etched on the tombstone of the human race.

My greatest fear is that the same petty jealousies, sectarian hatreds, racial passions, and silly national rivalries that slaughtered over 40 million people in two World Wars in the twentieth century may one day be played out with nuclear weapons.

Regrettably, our scientific skills have far outstripped the wisdom and compassion necessary to control this deadly, cosmic power. We are like spoiled infants playing with matches while floating on a swimming pool of gasoline.

To appreciate the power of Einstein's equation, remember that the essential ingredient in an atomic bomb is plutonium, one of the most toxic chemicals known to science. Only about ten pounds of plutonium, which is about the size of your fist, is required to attain "critical mass," the mass necessary for a nuclear detonation. Plutonium is aptly named after Pluto, the god of hell. A complete atomic bomb is no larger than a volleyball. A hydrogen bomb, which can be a thousand times more powerful than an atomic bomb, is no larger than a suitcase.

Now imagine a hydrogen bomb that is dropped on top of the Empire State Building. Within a millionth of a second, there is a burst of brilliant, blinding white light, brighter and hotter than the surface of the sun itself, which can destroy the eyes of anyone who witnesses it.

In less than a second, there will be a huge fireball, expanding to over a mile across, dwarfing the Empire State Building, which will be burnt to a cinder like a matchstick. In a few seconds, the fireball will create a powerful shock wave which will, like a giant hand from the sky, flatten Rockefeller Center and crush most of Manhattan, topple the Twin Towers of the World Trade Center and the Statue of Liberty, incinerate Wall Street, tear the Brooklyn Bridge apart, and pulverize large parts of the Bronx, Brooklyn, and Queens.

As the gigantic fireball rises into the sky, like the devil himself rising from hell, the intense heat will suck in huge hurricane-force winds, up to one hundred miles per hour. Thousands of tons of debris will be hurled into the wind, creating millions of deadly missiles and shards of glass which can rip apart anyone in their path.

The intense heat wave emanating from the fireball will ignite searing "firestorms," or raging infernos, out to one hundred miles from Manhattan, including large parts of Connecticut and New Jersey. People caught in these firestorms will suffocate and choke to death, the oxygen sucked right out of their lungs. Fires will rage uncontrollably for weeks.

The dirt and debris that was originally sucked into the fireball will also become highly radioactive, and radioactive particles will be spread by the wind hundreds of miles outside the New York metropolitan area. When it rains, the fallout will poison the reservoirs, create dangerous radioactive hot spots, and force the evacuation of entire towns.

Those fortunate enough to have escaped the heat, the shock wave, the firestorms, and the fallout will now face yet another problem: radiation sickness. Large clumps of hair will fall out when they brush their hair. Skin, like tissue paper, will slip off their flesh. Finally, there will be vomiting, fever, bleeding from the gums, and death.

Since almost 20 million people live within seventy miles of the Empire

State Building, the lives of almost 10 percent of the American population would be torn apart by the dropping of just one hydrogen bomb on New York.

Multiply the devastation of this one bomb by the number of nuclear warheads on this planet, fifty thousand. This is an almost inconceivable force, more than enough to extinguish all life on earth. Even a small nuclear war could cause environmental catastrophe. As few as one hundred hydrogen bombs incinerating one hundred major cities on the planet would be enough to create smoke clouds that would choke off the sunlight and plunge temperatures worldwide, creating a "nuclear winter." This could disrupt agriculture, destroy the major fertile areas around the world, and create worldwide famine and panic.

Perhaps the dinosaurs encountered a similar fate. Scientists have now identified a huge crater in the Yucatán Peninsula of Mexico, almost two hundred miles across, created when a huge comet or meteor slammed into the earth 64.9 million years ago. That titanic impact, like a nuclear war, was sufficient to darken the sun and wipe out most life forms on earth at that time.

Even if humanity manages to avoid a nuclear war, a nuclear accident, or the theft of a nuclear weapon, we have still paid an enormous price for the Cold War and the arms race: the trillions of dollars wasted on nuclear weapons.

One reason why the Soviet Union went bankrupt and collapsed is because of the enormous money and talent they wasted on nuclear weapons. This is the same reason why the United States is also in a historic decline. Real incomes of Americans are now falling, as the American Dream slips out of our grasp. For the first time in modern American history, the next generation will not live as well as the previous one.

Trillions of dollars that might have been used to finance productive industries to invigorate our sagging, aging economy were instead wasted on the Cold War. Our top scientists, like many of my friends, who might have created new industries to employ millions of unemployed Americans, instead worked on useless nuclear weapons. Now Europe and Asia are overtaking the United States in many key areas, such as consumer electronics, automobiles, and manufacturing, because their finest scientists and engineers are not drained off to work on nuclear weapons, as American scientists are. Their tax dollars go to generating new industries, not new missile systems.

The other problem is nuclear waste.

In the short term, government officials have said that it may cost upward of 500 billion dollars to clean up the hundreds of millions of gallons of high-level nuclear waste leaking from seventeen nuclear weapons plants around the country, many of them closed because of horrendous problems with nuclear contamination. These seventeen nuclear weapons sites sit like open sores on the planet Earth. They have polluted precious underground aquifers, exposed workers to dangerous levels of radiation, and sent radiation into people's homes.

In the long term, we still do not know what to do with nuclear waste, which will remain radioactive for millions of years. We sometimes forget that recorded history is only five thousand years old and that this country is only two centuries old. Who is going to guard our nuclear waste for hundreds of thousands of years to come? If the Neanderthals had had nuclear reactors, we would still be guarding their nuclear waste hundreds of thousands of years later.

So what lies ahead for humanity?

I sometimes am asked the interesting question: Is there intelligent life in outer space? Unfortunately, with our huge radio telescopes, we have scanned all the stars within one hundred light years of our planet, and we see no signs of intelligent life anywhere. But something is wrong, since we expect to find intelligent life in space simply because there are so many stars in the heavens.

My theory is that all intelligent life, emerging from the swamp after millions of years, will inevitably discover two things: first, plutonium and the ability to blow their planet apart; second, chemical pollution and the ability to poison air, food, and water. If we ever visit the stars, perhaps we will see only the ashes of cities pulverized by nuclear weapons, or the thick pollution that destroyed their atmospheres and oceans.

So we stand at the final crossroads. Our civilization, like perhaps millions of other civilizations in space, is now being tested. One path leads to destruction, the other path to a new golden age. Of all the generations of humans who have walked the surface of the earth, the generation now alive is by far the most important, since we can, for the first time, destroy all life on earth. Will we have the wisdom and foresight to control the racial, sectarian, and national passions that might have destroyed intelligent life in outer space? I hope so, and I hope that everyone who reads this will become part of the historic movement to destroy these weapons forever and usher in humanity's golden age.

Rafal Olbinski

Peter Catalanotto

✋ The Dayspring

by Martin Waddell

A stone hero lay in a cathedral, Major Arbuthnot, V.C., surrounded by flags and by drums.

In a stall on the wall above Major Arbuthnot, V.C., were John William Lennox and Maud, carved in wood.

All day the cathedral was busy, but at night when the people had gone, there was quiet, and peace.

Then, one night, with a roar and a shake, the world B R O K E!

In the mess and the rubble lay John William Lennox and Maud. There was no more of Major Arbuthnot. He'd gone west, with the rest.

"What's all this about then, Johnny?" asked Maud, sitting up.

"Well, I'm bothered," said John William Lennox. "You're *talking*!"

"It's right queer, ain't it?" said Maud. "I thought I was just made of wood."

"It was good wood," said John William Lennox, "and old."

"But that doesn't explain you and me talking!" said Maud.

They got up and shook themselves down and looked all about them at the ruins.

"Is anyone there?" shouted John William Lennox.

"Please help us!" cried Maud.

Nobody came. Nothing stirred. They clung close together in the dirt and the dust, John William Lennox and Maud.

"We're out on our own, lass!" said John William Lennox.

"I don't like it, our Johnny," said Maud. "What do we think we're about?"

"I haven't a clue, lass," said John William Lennox, "but I think, pretty soon, we'll find out." They both shouted again, but nobody came.

"Maybe it's *Him*," said John William Lennox. "Happen He's made a mistake, and blowed the lot up."

"I don't think He'd do that," said Maud. "It was *them*, and their soldiers and guns."

31

ribbons covered with hyacinth flowers. On feast days, she wore a petticoat of colored embroidery that seemed to float when she went happily dancing off to school over the hills and brooks, or when she rested under the generous shade of an Ombú tree.

One day a couple came from North America with a boy the same age as Marisol. They had reached the village between the mountain range and the sea to learn more about the happy people who lived there, wrote on green chalkboards, and liked to sing. Also, the boy wanted to learn Spanish. The couple invited Marisol to spend some time in the northern country. Marisol's mother was kind to let her daughter fly in a plane that looked like a green bird with gigantic wings that carried her toward the north and the land where the winters and the meadows are covered with frost.

A few days before she left, Marisol's friends from school had many parties for her. The teacher gave her a pencil decorated with the feathers of a bird from a place called Chinclo. Three of her friends prepared a dance just for Marisol, and gave it to her as a gift. Some other friends gave her flower garlands so she would remember the fragrance of the valleys and the color of the hills of her homeland.

Marisol Antipán put a small handful of dirt inside her pocket from the place where she first saw the light of day. Then she wrapped up her first bouquet of hyacinths to remember the time her mother let her grow her hair of dark night and make it look pretty with such sweet-smelling flowers.

When she reached the country in the north, she was amazed at all the shoes, alarm clocks, and televisions. But what was truly beautiful was the huge yellow school bus that came faithfully to her block every morning at eight o'clock to pick her up.

Marisol Antipán was astonished the first day she saw the yellow bus. She got confused and thought it was an enormous animal like a moving jaguar or a camel. And for a long time she thought the bus was a great big sunflower with wheels to make it fly.

Marisol woke up with an electric alarm clock that had a face like a mouse. She put on her new red shoes. They were very different from the shoes made of cornhusks. She didn't eat the tortillas her mother used to knead in the outdoor oven. So she served herself some alphabet cereal, and without realizing it, she saw the huge yellow sunflower waiting for her right on time.

A boy sat beside her and took her by the hand. Then he said to her, "This is a yellow bus." And Marisol told him in her new English, "Yes, like a big sun."

Marisol's greatest joy during her short stay in the north was to ride to school on the yellow sunflower. She would sit beside the boy who was waiting for her and had saved her a seat. Then, in English, he would teach Marisol the words she liked best: *love, friendship*, and *peace*. She also learned to say "summer," although she sadly found out that the bus wouldn't come to her house in the summer, because then it would be resting in the yellow meadows behind the corn fields until the next fall.

When Marisol Antipán returned to her village and her school, she told her friends about the yellow bus that seemed to smile and have a very yellow nose, sometimes, or even be a gigantic flower. The children became excited and they began to repeat the words Marisol taught them in English, "Yellow bus, yellow bus."

Marisol Antipán would remember the yellow bus. She would remember the boy who shared the world with her in English every morning and taught her how to say *peace, summer*, and *love*. She also remembered her red shoes and kept them next to the eucalyptus branches her mother had placed under her bed to cure colds and fill the house with the beautiful wood aromas the forests have. Often, when the first stars would cover the southern hemisphere's sky like a sparkling blanket, Marisol Antipán would remember the yellow bus like a giant sunflower or a golden armadillo. She was happy thinking about the time long ago that tasted of magic.

Marisol Antipán still got up with the hummingbirds and the thrushes. After school she would still come home with the iguanas and lizards, repeating the alphabet on sunny and rainy days. But in her heart, she would always remember when the yellow bus waited for her every morning and when her friend gave her his hand in a new language.

In the evening, Marisol's mother would put eucalyptus branches under her bed because they smelled good and gave good dreams. Marisol went to sleep

Enrique O. Sanchez

with her hands wrapped around the alarm clock with a mouse's face that her friend in the north had given her.

Before she said good night, Marisol would say the words of peace out loud that she had learned in the new language. As soon as she said the words, *love*, *friendship*, and *peace*, Marisol Antipán would go to sleep. Then she would go deeply into the enchanted garden of dreams that didn't have any countries or borders—only the winged dreams of peace.

Umareru ("To Be Born") by Setsu Kunii

❧ To a Child of War

by Walter Dean Myers

If you can but wait
Behind those wide Methuselah eyes
For yet another heartbeat
I will come with myrrh,
Sweet incense
And burnt oranges
Bright soup bowls of laughter
And furry dreams to run
Your fingers through
If you can but wait

40

If only you will not grow
Hard edged too soon
I will come with miles
Of wonder yarn
To leash your mourning
My trembling, bloody hands
Will steady you a same/grief longer
And my glad song will croak against
The pale brilliance of the dead moon
If you can but wait

If you can but wait
There in your hand-me-down shadows
I will take you to a secret garden
Where snowflakes dance
With rainbows
And lobsters waltz with willow trees
And other children laugh, and laugh
And other children laugh
If you can but wait
With sweet forgiveness

James E. Ransome

ꙅ Sky

Written and illustrated by Junko Morimoto

When I was a child,
my country was in war.
And I was afraid of the SKY . . .
was always looking for an enemy plane.

Each time the siren sounded,
I ran for a shelter.
My body trembled in the
small dark pit.

When the moon grew,
I was afraid. . . .

They can see my town.
They can see my house.
They can see me!
Nowhere to hide from the
deadly plane.

42

One morning,
I heard a sound of airplane,
above my head in the *SKY* . . .
I thought it was B29.

When I stood up,
the blast of light struck me.
The intense heat wrapped my body.
I was dazed and frozen.

Then the whole house was shaken.
Everything blew up.
I screamed.
The light collapsed and
I fell into darkness.

I thought "Bomb hit me . . ."
I thought "I'm dying . . ."
I sank deeply into the pitch darkness.

Gradually the light returned,
together with the echoes of
millions of people screaming around me.
And I saw the SKY above me.

I was sitting under a fallen beam.
The house was gone.
I crawled out in the dust.
Then, I saw that the entire city was flattened.

My family left everything behind
and ran away from the chasing fire.
I saw the people whose skin
was hanging down from their fingertips.

I saw a baby crying by
the dead mother.
It was hopeless.
It was desperate.

When the peace finally came,
I was hungry. . . .
I survived intense fever.
My father survived burnt face.
At least we were alive.

I saw the messages scratched
on a concrete wall. . . .
"*Yoshie Yamamoto* thirteen years old.
If anybody knows what happened to my daughter
please let me know."

Standing in the middle of nothingness,
I realized
what horror human beings can create.

Autumn came,
it started getting colder.
"What should I wear?"
But in the chilly air,
I was looking up at the *SKY* . . .
And the *SKY* was finally safe and free.

ᔛ School Caps (A True Story)
by Kyoko Mori

June, 1990. My aunt, Michiyo, and I are visiting the Peace Memorial Park in Hiroshima, almost forty-five years after the atomic bomb exploded here. Neither of us remembers that day. She was only a baby, living in another city. I had not been born yet.

The rain begins as soon as we enter the park—not a downpour, but the early-summer rain that falls like handfuls of long threads. Our path weaves among many memorial statues and plaques. The largest one is a rock surrounded by flowers that is dedicated to all the people who died in the bombing. The prayer carved on it says, "Please rest in peace. The mistake will not be repeated."

At the end of our path, Michiyo and I go into the memorial museum. Inside the small exhibit rooms, the shelves are lined with things saved from the day of the bomb: watches that stopped at the exact moment of the explosion, burned clothing of the victims, broken windows, a piano with its wires snapped. Large photographs show collapsed buildings and injured people. Michiyo has visited here many times before, because she and Uncle Shiro, my mother's younger brother, live in Hiroshima and their guests often want to see the museum. Still, her face looks sad and serious. We don't talk as we move from one room to the next.

In the third room, we catch up with about twenty schoolchildren in navy blue uniforms. They are standing in orderly double rows while their teacher, a young man, points at the various things on the wall and explains what they were. The students are all boys, no older than second or third grade.

When the teacher is done, we follow the group into the next room, which is very dark. In a roped-off area, two mannequins, mother and daughter, are posed under an eerie orange sky. The mannequins' kimonos are tattered and singed. Cuts and burns mark their faces. Their feet are covered with ashes and rubble. A hush falls over the children ahead of us. They keep walking in their double rows, staring straight ahead. Their heads, under the navy blue uniform caps, scarcely move to either side.

Those caps, made of felt except for the wide black bill, are a sign of discipline. They go with the navy blue blazers with brass buttons, the matching trousers, and the white shirts that must be ironed and starched for weekly inspections. The uniforms have not changed since before the War, when my father's younger brother, Tsuyoshi, was in middle school. I never met Tsuyoshi. I only know two stories about him, one of which is about his school cap.

In 1945, Tsuyoshi lived in Hiroshima with his parents and his sister, Akiko. At his school, classes were often canceled and the students taken to factories to make guns, bullets, and soldiers' uniforms. Young men—only a few years older than the students—had gone to fight. Everyone had to help their country win the war, Tsuyoshi was told.

On the morning of the atomic explosion, Tsuyoshi was in a factory downtown. His parents and Akiko were at their home in the suburbs. When they heard about the bomb, they immediately set out to look for Tsuyoshi. The factory where he had been working was unrecognizable. The downtown was full of burned buildings, hurt and dying people stumbling around. There was no sign of Tsuyoshi or his classmates. Still, they kept looking every day, rising early to walk all over the city and coming home at dusk.

One evening in the second week of their search, the family returned home to find an old man at their gate. The stranger walked straight up to my grandmother, Kiku, bowed deeply, and handed her a blue school cap. Kiku turned it over. On the inside rim, she found Tsuyoshi's name and address, which she had embroidered for him. Kiku stared at the stitches, unable to speak. The man bowed again, this time also to my grandfather and to Akiko, who were standing behind Kiku.

"There was nothing I could do for your son," the man said in a choked-up voice. He had met Tsuyoshi the day after the bomb, when both of them were walking by one of the rivers, looking for help. A few hours later, Tsuyoshi fell down from exhaustion and died. All around them, people were dying. The man, who was burned and sick, had no choice but to go on. He took Tsuyoshi's cap, hoping to look for his family later.

"The moment I saw you," he said to Kiku, "I knew I had come to the right house. Your son looked very much like you."

A few weeks later, the family moved back to Kyoto to join my father, who

was going to high school there. They never went back to Hiroshima, even to see the memorial park and the museum.

⌇

The last room of the museum has watercolor pictures painted by the survivors of the bomb. They show fire, dead bodies, rivers full of blood. At the door, watching the children file out ahead of us, I think of the children during the war.

At my mother's middle school, the principal unveiled the emperor's picture after his morning lecture. The students had to close their eyes as soon as the veil was lifted. Seeing the emperor's holy likeness, they were told, would blind them. My mother kept her eyes open and found out that she did not become blind.

Though my mother was able to discover the lie about the emperor's picture, she believed in many things that later turned out not to be true. When she and her classmates went to factories to sew the soldiers' uniforms, she believed that the Japanese soldiers were like pure white cherry blossoms falling for their country. She felt great pride in helping them carry on a war that she was taught was necessary. Every day on the radio she heard patriotic songs and felt moved

48

Keiko Narahashi

by the sacrifices people were making to win the war. She had no idea of the terrible things the Japanese troops were doing to people in Korea, in China, all over Asia. She knew nothing about what had caused the war, why it was necessary. Swept away by her feelings, she did not learn to ask the right questions. She came to regret that very much.

In their somber blue uniforms, the children keep walking in their double rows through the park. Walking behind them, I am not sure if we have made much progress since my mother's time. To be sure, the children now are taught that war is bad. But that isn't enough. The anti-war message now appeals only to our feelings, just as the pro-war message had appealed to my mother's feelings. Though the exhibit of the museum promotes peace, it still does not encourage us to ask questions: why so many countries decided to resort to the violence and destruction that led to the Second World War, how each country was responsible. If I were eight or nine, a Japanese child, I would go away from this museum thinking of my country as a helpless victim. I would not know that we, too, had destroyed other people and their homes. I would know little more than my mother had.

Michiyo and I retrace our steps on the path, past the largest memorial stone. Again, I read the prayer carved on it. "Please rest in peace. The mistake will not be repeated." I am disturbed by the vague words. What do we mean by the mistake? Another world war? The atomic bomb? Or all war? And whose mistake was it anyway?

The saddest thing about Tsuyoshi's death is that he died for the wrong cause. He was in a factory making bullets for the soldiers who were killing other people somewhere else. That is not his fault in a direct way; he did not deserve to die for that. Still, he died believing in war, working in his small way to continue it. If I look away from that painful fact, I would not be doing him justice.

If I could carve a prayer on the memorial stone, I would say, "Please rest in peace. We understand your tragedy. You were killed in the war you believed in without thinking. We promise to ask the right questions, to think critically, to find peaceful solutions to problems so that we will not use violence against other people and they will not use it against us. We will not repeat your mistake. You have taught us this."

Perhaps that would be less poetic and much too long to fit on the rock. Still, if Tsuyoshi were alive, I think he would approve.

ॐ

The second story I know about Tsuyoshi is about his counting stars. When Tsuyoshi was in fourth grade, he began to have trouble reading the blackboard. He found himself squinting at his books. Right away, he went to see a doctor.

"You are becoming nearsighted," the doctor told him. "But you are very young. It may not be too late to improve your eyesight, to train yourself to see better again. Every night before you go to bed, look at the sky and try to count the stars."

For a month, Tsuyoshi counted the stars for half an hour before going to bed. When he went back to the doctor, he did not need glasses.

I hope that is what he would have wanted me to remember: our nearsightedness, caught in time, can be reversed. I hope, too, that he enjoyed counting the stars, even if he did it just to make his eyes better. His life was short. I want to believe that he found as much beauty in it as possible.

୬ I Dreaded December 7

by Ken Mochizuki

I hated every December 7.

I hated it especially when that day landed on a weekday, and I would have to leave home and go to school.

My friends didn't act so friendly on that day, and other kids at school, who had nothing against me at any other time, did then.

I heard the same stuff all day at school on December 7: "The Japs bombed Pearl Harbor!" "Your country bombed Pearl Harbor!" While I was walking home from school, guys who played with me the 364 other days of the year zoomed at me in a formation of bikes, pumping their pedals furiously, going "Rat-tat-tat-tat! Got another Jap!" as they swished past.

What are they mad at me for? I always wondered. I wasn't alive when Pearl Harbor happened. I've never even been to Japan.

Another December 7 drew near, but this year was different because Uncle Tad came.

All I knew was that Uncle Tad was born here in the U.S.A., like Mom and Dad were. But Uncle Tad had gone to Japan to work and when World War II broke out he got stuck there. My parents never said exactly what happened to him, other than that he got injured in the war somehow.

He showed up for Thanksgiving at our house. Although Mom warned me not to stare at his face, I couldn't help it. His face wasn't scary. It's just that I was, in a weird way, fascinated. What could have blackened and melted just one side?

At the dinner table, I just about flew out of my seat when Uncle Tad suddenly turned to me and said, "You're probably wondering what happened to my face."

He told me. He had two lives, he said. The first ended on August 6, 1945. The second began when people never stopped staring at his face.

He said he was lucky to be driving a car that morning and lucky to be alive.

Dom Lee

Working for a news agency in Japan, he saw how most cities in Japan had been bombed into nothing—blocks and blocks of burned buildings. He drove into Hiroshima to report on what the people there thought about why their large city had never been bombed.

With his car window open on another hot, sunny morning, he heard the city's air raid siren, followed by the all-clear siren not too long after.

All of a sudden, a blinding flash went off in front of him, as though the biggest flashbulb in the world had popped, blue and brighter than the sun on a clear day. Instinct screamed at him to turn around, drive away as fast as he could. He slammed on the brakes; his car's tires screeched to make the quick U-turn. Right in the middle of the turn, the car window on his side exploded, shattering as it caved in. The unstoppable light burst through; with searing pain it scorched the side of his face facing the flash.

Fortunately, he was able to speed away. He kept going as far as he could until the car ran out of gas, Uncle Tad said at the dinner table. And that's the last he said about it. He gave me that look grownups sometimes give: a stare from the backs of their eyes that says they don't want to talk about something anymore and they have told you all you need to know.

I hoped Uncle Tad would stay in town through December 7. He could probably tell those kids a thing or two. But he had to go before then.

I had to do it by myself. On that day, the kids hassled me as expected. "Your country bombed Pearl Harbor!"

I yelled back: "No! My country bombed Hiroshima!"

ᔓ A Fountain of Peace

by Edwidge Danticat

Jean Durandisse

The island of Fontaine-de-Paix in Haiti is shaped exactly like a gorgeous, breathtaking whale. I will tell you how this came to be.

There has always been fighting in Haiti: battles, wars, and all kinds of various strife. One day while looking across the ocean, Mother Africa was sad.

"My children in Haiti have been fighting one another for generations," she said. "They have fought one another for food. They have fought one another for land. They have fought one another for power. The men have fought the women. The young have fought the old. The rich have fought the poor. The ones who are light-skinned have fought the ones who are dark-skinned. The

55

ones who are dark-skinned have fought the ones who are light-skinned. The ones who live in the cities have fought with the ones who live in the countryside. It is time I put an end to this."

To solve this problem, Mother Africa met with a trio of Haitian deities called *loas*. She met with Ogoun, the Haitian *loa* of war; Agwé, the master of the ocean; and Erzulie, the goddess of love.

"Ogoun, you have been working too hard," Mother Africa said to the Haitian *loa* of war. "There is so much fighting among my children in Haiti. What should I do to bring them peace?"

"I would drop a bolt of red-blood fire lightning among them," Ogoun said. "If they are fighting the forces of the universe, then they cannot fight each other."

"But this bolt of red-blood fire lightning might cause confusion," said Mother Africa with concern. "And in the confusion we might harm some of them unintentionally. Besides, they might think themselves at war with the forces of the universe and this would never lead to peace."

"I partly agree with Ogoun," said Agwé, master of the ocean. "In order for them to have peace, we have to send them some kind of signal, something that will guide them to peace."

"I would send them the formula for peace," suggested Erzulie, the Haitian goddess of love. "You must find a way to remind them that peace means tranquility and harmony, which can only come through love."

The next day, Mother Africa was strolling by the sea when she saw the largest, most gorgeous, breathtaking whale that she had ever seen. She remembered what Erzulie, the Haitian goddess of love, had said, and this gave her a wonderful idea.

"I will write the formula for peace in a letter," she said, "and send that letter to my children in Haiti, and this whale will be the one to carry my message.

"Most beautiful daughter of the sea," called Mother Africa to the whale, "I need to ask your help in a most important matter."

"I am always ready to serve you, Madam," said the whale. "I am most at your service."

"I need you to take a message to my children in Haiti," Mother Africa said. "They have been at war with one another for years and I need to send them a formula for peace."

"I will do my best to serve," the whale said.

"I know the journey is long," Mother Africa said. "Haiti is far away and you may get tired, but this is a most important mission. My children in Haiti need to receive this message. They need to understand."

Mother Africa wrote down the formula for peace in a letter. She took her time to write this very clearly: that peace means tranquility and harmony, which can only come through love.

After writing the message, Mother Africa handed it to the whale.

"Godspeed," she said to the whale as the whale went on her way.

All through the whale's journey, the sea was calm and soothing. The whale raced ahead with no difficulty. However, the shores of Mother Africa are far from the shores of Haiti and soon the whale became very tired.

"I want to stay awake," the whale thought, "but I am so tired that I must rest. I will stop here near this plot of land and rest for a while before moving on."

The whale did not realize that the place where she was taking her rest was just off the coast of Haiti. She moved her way to the shore and attached her body to a beach to rest for a while.

After her very long journey, the whale was so tired that she slept for days and months and even to this day has not yet woken up. As she sleeps, with each breath she blows a stream of water up in the air, in such a way that it looks like a water fountain.

The Haitians who live nearby noticed this curious mount that had risen on their beach and the pretty water fountain that came with it. They moved their homes on top of the whale's back and built a fishing village there.

Across the ocean, Mother Africa waits with a more rested heart, knowing that one day very soon the whale will wake up from her sleep to complete her mission, giving the people of Haiti their formula for peace.

"On that day when the whale wakes up from its rest, my children in Haiti will finally have peace," Mother Africa says. And because of this, she has named the area where the whale is sleeping Fontaine-de-Paix, which in our language means "Fountain of Peace." And this is how the island of Fontaine-de-Paix came to have that name.

ᔓ Tomorrow When Everything Will Be All Right

by Bent Haller
Translated from the Danish by Paulette Møller

The boy and the girl were with their family when the soldiers came in their trucks. The boy, who was the eldest, helped the girl indoors. Of course he was scared when they set fire to the house, but he was with Mom and Dad and the others. As they ran across the field his only thought was that they should all reach the trees in safety.

The girl could not understand. She was only five years old. She pointed to the black clouds and said, "Rain." She did not understand why the rain did not come. She did not understand why they had to run.

The boy did not understand either, not fully, because no one had time to explain. They had no time to gather up any of their belongings, not even the girl's doll.

"I can make you a new doll, with white hair," he said. He made her think about something else. While they walked to escape from the soldiers, he told her a story about a clown with blue eyes and a white face. She laughed when he pretended to fall.

He was not so scared now, because he was walking together with Mom and Dad and the others.

"Tomorrow everything will be all right again," said the boy.

They walked for days, and it was difficult to find food. They met up with more people all the time, and always there were soldiers in trucks. Always there were burning skies in the night.

"But tomorrow the fires will be put out," said the boy.

The girl began to sing to herself. She believed what he told her. Always. She laughed and danced when she saw the sun rise.

"Look here," said the boy, giving her a stick he had whittled. "This is a doll with white hair." And he went on telling stories about the doll with white hair until she discovered that it *was* a doll with white hair.

The boy and the girl were with their family when the soldiers appeared early

Paul Hunt

one morning in their trucks. The boy ran after the others, holding the girl by the hand. She did not cry even though she was scared. She had her doil.

When they had been running for a while, they again saw black smoke in the sky. The girl said, "Where are Mom and Dad?"

"They have run on ahead," said the boy. "Tomorrow we'll get to the place where they are."

"Is tomorrow far?" she asked.

"If we don't keep on walking," said the boy, "we'll never get to tomorrow."

Sometimes he had to leave her. It was hard to find food. He tried begging. He tried stealing. He tried everything, and whatever he could get hold of he took back to the place where the girl was waiting.

"Just take it," he said, "I've eaten."

The boy explained to the girl that they were not alone, for there were people all around them, even some they once knew.

"Look," he said, "they are all waiting for tomorrow."

It was always easy to know where the soldiers were. When they had finished their work they drove on to the next place. They traveled swiftly. They were skilled, they did their work with thoroughness, but that was not something the boy could talk to the girl about. He had to talk about something else. About tomorrow.

At night she shivered with cold, but he had no clothes to give her. Instead he held her close to him and said, "I'll tell you a story."

He told her a story about two children who were lost and couldn't find their mother and father. But then they were found again.

"The clown with the white face helped them," he said, rolling his eyes dramatically. That made her laugh again.

He drew in the sand with a stick. An ear of corn. He told her to eat it. She played that she was full. Then she fell asleep while he sat and brushed the flies away.

"Tomorrow," he whispered.

They were together when the soldiers came back, but this time the girl was prepared. She remembered the doll with white hair, which was a stick the boy had whittled. She hugged it close.

"When?" she asked again.

And he answered, "Tomorrow. It's certain."

It got more and more difficult for the boy to find food. And harder to keep her warm at night. They had become separated from the people they once knew. Now there were only strangers around them. After a night when birds had screeched above them, they got to a place where there were no other people at all.

"If only you could go a bit farther," said the boy, "it'll soon be tomorrow."

It got harder and harder for the boy to tell her the story of the two children who got lost. He wanted to, but his voice had grown so weak.

"It's because I've got a sore throat," he whispered.

He also had difficulty drawing ears of corn. His drawings had become lopsided and incomprehensible.

"But tomorrow we'll have plenty of food," he said stubbornly.

Next morning when the soldiers came, the boy did not get up. So the girl sat still, hugging the doll with white hair. One of the soldiers, casting the biggest shadow she had ever seen in her whole life, stood looking at them. Then he walked away. He was a friendly soldier. She raised her hand and waved.

The boy said he was tired. But that she should go on.

"They are close by," he said, "I know they are."

At first the girl would not go on alone, because she did not know what being alone was like.

"But you are not alone," he said, "you've got the doll with white hair. Listen! Can't you hear them calling?"

She nodded. She had the doll with white hair. And when the sun rose she really could hear their voices. Louder and louder. Exactly like he said.

Nancy Carpenter

ᔐ Letters from Baghdad

by Barbara Bedway

January 5, 1990

Dear Margaret,

Mother and I stopped at the Church of the Virgin and St. Paul to pray for peace. The church still had its Christmas tree up, covered in tinsel, with red, yellow, blue, and green lights blinking on and off in the darkness. It seems a million years ago that we got your Christmas card. Mother and I pray every day our country will withdraw from Kuwait, so that we will not have war. Margaret, please pray too.

Everyone is buying as much food as they can. The basement of our house— do you remember how we liked to play cards there because it was cool and eat pistachio nuts out of a sack on the floor?—Well, now it's full of barrels holding pistachios and raisins and wheat, and the freezer is full to bursting with lamb and chickens. You could fall over the stacks of toilet paper and tea and spaghetti and my brother's cigarette cartons. Everyone puts masking tape on the windows, for when the bombs come. Do you think it will really happen?

Mother had a good idea for how I can keep up my English. We speak Arabic downstairs, and only English upstairs! It's fun, because I remember how you and I would sit on my bed and brush each other's hair and talk about clothes and boys and music. I still remember all the words to Paula Abdul's "Forever Your Girl." Sometimes I pretend it's you I am talking to upstairs, though Adnan makes fun of me.

Are you keeping up with your Arabic? Remember how Adnan taught you to say *Mish melleh*, "No problem," whenever you were asked something and you didn't understand? Sometimes, when the news is scary and the house looks so gloomy with windows taped shut, I think about your visit last summer and wonder if I will ever get to visit you in America. I would like to be an archaeologist like your father when I grow up, and travel all over the world like he does.

May 25, 1991

Dear Margaret,

Your letter from months ago arrived at last. I read it to Adnan in the hospital, and I think that was a smile, underneath his bandages. He has lost one eye and the fingers of his right hand. We know that he is lucky, lucky to be alive, but still my mother cries over him when she visits. He likes me to sing the songs you taught me last summer, "Forever Your Girl" and "Everlasting Love" and "If You Don't Know Me by Now." We will take him home soon because the hospital needs the space for others, and they are running out of his medicine, too. If you ask Adnan how we will find more medicine, or pay for food, you can guess what his answer will be: *Mish melleh*, he says, but I know better now.

Nobuhiko Yabuki

Murv Jacob

ᦔ Rabbit Foot: A Story of the Peacemaker

Told by Joseph Bruchac

I was first taught this story many years ago by Mohawk elder Tenanetorens/Ray Fadden at his Six Nations Indian Museum in Onchlota, New York. It is only one of a long cycle of stories about the coming of the Peacemaker to the Iroquois people and the eventual formation of their Great League of Peace.

Many hundreds of years ago
before the Europeans came
the Five Nations of the Iroquois,
Mohawk and Oneida, Onondaga, Cayuga and Seneca,
were always at war with one another.

Although they had a common culture
and languages that were much the same
no longer did they remember
they had been taught to live
as sisters and brothers.

Once they had shared the beautiful land
from Niagara to the eastern mountains,
but now only revenge was in their hearts
and blood feuds had made every trail
a path leading to war.

So it was that the Great Creator
sent once again a messenger,
a man who became known
to all of the Five Nations
by the name of the Peacemaker.

To help the people once again
make their minds straight
he told them stories
about peace and war.
This is one of his tales.

Once there was a boy named Rabbit Foot.
He was always looking and listening.
He knew how to talk to the animals
so the animals would talk to him.

One day as he walked out in the woods
he heard the sound of a great struggle
coming from a clearing just over the hill.
So he climbed that hilltop to look down.

What he saw surprised him.
There was a great snake
coiled in a circle.
It had caught a huge frog
and although the frog struggled
the snake was slowly swallowing its legs.

Rabbit Foot came closer
and spoke to the frog.
"He has really got you, my friend."
The frog looked up at Rabbit Foot.
"Wa'he! That is so," the frog said.

Rabbit Foot nodded, then said to the frog,
"Do you see the snake's tail there,
just in front of your mouth?
Why not do to him what he's doing to you?"

Then the huge frog reached out
and grabbed the snake's tail.
He began to stuff it into his mouth
as Rabbit Foot watched both of them.

The snake swallowed more of the frog
the frog swallowed more of the snake
and the circle got smaller and smaller
until both of them swallowed one last time
and just like that, they both were gone.

They had eaten each other,
the Peacemaker said.
And in much the same way,
unless you give up war
and learn to live together in peace,
that also will happen to you.

Jerry Pinkney

✌ The Dissenters

by Milton Meltzer

Men and women have resisted the call to violent action in various ways throughout the history of the United States, from the colonial wars and the Revolution down to the many conflicts that have bled millions in this century. The Quakers were among the first dissenters to bring pacifism to America. George Fox, an English cobbler, formed the Society of Friends, called Quakers, in the 1600s. They stood firmly against all wars, whether religious or worldly, and many suffered for their beliefs.

Labeled a "fanatical sect," they were often imprisoned. But persecution did not shatter their movement. They grew rapidly, drawing in people of all social classes and levels of learning. (Among them was William Penn, who established Pennsylvania as a home in America for the new sect.) Women took a prominent part early in the movement. If God was in everyone, then women as well as men could be chosen by the Inner Light to be ministers, they believed.

For the Friends, pacifism was not a retreat from the world. Wherever they lived they opposed, for reasons of conscience, militia drills, oath-taking, jury service, and religious taxes. As a number of Quakers made their homes in the new settlements of America, they swiftly discovered that this new America was no peaceful paradise. From the first, the reality was conflict between whites and Native Americans. The Puritan colonists, for instance, believed the Indians were hardly human and therefore the land they lived upon was open territory to be grabbed at will. But the Quakers would not take up arms against the Indians, and for refusing the command to fight they were treated harshly.

Refusal by a Quaker to serve in the colonial militia brought about the first recorded case of an American persecuted for conscientious objection. In 1658 Richard Keene, a Maryland Quaker, refused to be trained as a soldier. Fining him heavily, the angry sheriff drew his cutlass and struck young Keene on the shoulder, saying, "You dog! I could find in my heart to split your brains!"

An early trial of Quaker peace beliefs in Massachusetts came during the war with the Indians. The colony passed a law that imprisoned anyone who refused to bear arms or was unwilling to pay a fine in place of service. The Quaker John Smith, aged twenty-two, was called to join the militia in 1703. He refused, and was tried, and was fined. When he would not pay the fine, he was sentenced to hard labor in the fort at Boston for as long as would pay the fine and costs. The judge said "only ignorance and a perverse nature" could lead anyone to refuse to fight the enemy. Smith replied that "It was not obstinacy, but duty to God, according to conscience, and religious persuasion" which prevailed with him "to refuse to bear arms, or learn war."

Sent to the fort, Smith refused to perform military labor. After four months, the governor released him. He then joined the crew of a Quaker merchant's ship bound for England. When it docked at Plymouth he was seized by the British for service in the royal navy. At sea, a French ship gave them battle, and Smith was placed at a gun and ordered to fire. Again he refused because on the naval vessel this would be war work. An enraged officer had him whipped savagely. For thirteen months at sea his life was made hell, until the ship returned to Plymouth and the captain said he never wanted to see this reluctant sailor again.

The question always raised for conscientious objectors is: Would you fight if your country were attacked? To Quakers like John Woolman, a tailor from New Jersey, a nonviolent world was their hope. Woolman saw peace as a total way of life, not just a special interest of the Quakers. In his journal he wrote:

> It requires great self-denial and resignation of ourselves to God to attain that state wherein we can freely cease from fighting when wrongfully invaded, if by our fighting there was a probability of overcoming the invaders. Whoever rightly attains to it, does in some degree feel that spirit in which our Redeemer gave his life for us.

When people ask this question, they are really suggesting that willingness to fight is a test of patriotism. Conscientious objectors love their country as much as anybody else. By saying no to war, they speak out of the deep conviction that killing is wrong no matter what the circumstances.

Homage by Peter E. Clarke

❧ The Grandmother with Her Own Bomb

by Katherine Paterson

When the bomb came through the roof, Bragantosova was sure she was dead. I guess you don't hear anything when you're dead, she thought, because I never heard any explosion. And where was the fire? She must have died and gone to heaven. She opened her eyes and peeked around. Heaven seemed more like her old room in the tiny house in the Russian village where she had lived alone since her husband went off to war and her old parents had died.

Something was wrong, though. She could see the stars. There they were, blinking merrily in the dark sky. She wasn't dead. She was in her own house, but there was an enormous hole in her ceiling. She climbed out of bed to take a better look and caught herself just before she stumbled into another giant opening at her feet.

Bragantosova stepped back and crouched down on all fours. It was too dark to see much. But there, look. She could see a gleam of metal in her cellar. She had no flashlight and she was afraid to light a match. There was nothing to do but wait until morning. She crawled back to her bed and climbed in.

There was no hope of sleep. She wondered if she should leave. Was it dangerous to stay there with what must be a bomb underneath her house? She should have gone to the bomb shelter when she first heard the sirens the night before, but she'd just been too tired to move. She was still tired. If the bomb hadn't exploded when it fell, surely she was safe for a few hours. Still, it was impossible to sleep with a visitor like that in the cellar.

As soon as it was light, Bragantosova climbed down and crawled over to the hole. Yes, there was no doubt. A bomb had fallen through her roof, gone straight through the floor of her bedroom, and landed in the cellar. She crawled around the hole to the bureau and got her clothes and her shawl. She must notify the police at once. Should the bomb explode it would not only kill her, but a lot of the neighbors as well.

She ran down the street to the police station and got in a long line of people

Diana Bryan

waiting to talk to the officer in charge. When Bragantosova's turn came, she told the officer on duty the whole story. As she talked the officer pursed his lips and tapped his fingers impatiently on the desk. "Fell through your roof and landed in the cellar, you say?"

"Yes, just as I said. Right through the bedroom ceiling."

"And where did you say you were?" he asked.

"I was in bed on the other side of the room."

He cocked his head. "In bed?"

"I know I should have gone to the shelter, but . . ."

"You were just lying there when a great big bad bomb fell right through the ceiling past your bed and into the turnip pile in your cellar?"

"Yes," she said. "Only there are no turnips in my cellar. Food is scarce, you know."

"Well, that's good," he said. "The big bad bomb didn't hurt anything then, did it? Next . . ."

"Wait," cried Bragantosova. "Isn't it dangerous . . . ?" But no one was listening. The man who was next pushed her aside and began to tell his story to the officer.

What could she do? She had nowhere to go but home, so home she went. She took apart an empty cabinet in the kitchen, got a ladder and hammer and nails, and climbed up and patched her roof. There was nothing left with which to patch the bedroom floor. She left it as it was for a few days, but it was dangerous walking around a gaping hole in the dark, so finally she shoved her bed across the floor to cover the crater.

From time to time she would go down to the police station and tell the officer in charge about the bomb. She felt responsible. She was very fond of the neighborhood children. She wouldn't want anything to happen to them because she had failed to warn the authorities. But every time she tried, the results were the same. No one believed her.

Eventually, the war ended. Bragantosova's husband never came home. She began to grow old. The more time passed, the less likely her story seemed. The policemen could hardly keep a straight face when she'd come through the door of the station. "Oh, don't make fun of her," one of the kinder ones said. "She's just trying to get one of those nice apartments in the new buildings that are going up. Can you blame her?" The children she had worried about grew up and had their own children—children who laughed when they saw her going down the street. "There goes the grandmother with her own bomb!" they would say.

Finally, forty-three years after she had first pulled her bed over the bomb hole, workmen came into the neighborhood to lay telephone cable. Before they began digging, they posted signs: "Anyone with knowledge of buried explosives is required to report them to the police."

Once more, Bragantosova put on her shawl and made her way to the police station. Now the law demanded that all reports be checked out, so the next day a brash young lieutenant appeared at Bragantosova's front door.

"Where's your bomb, Grandma?" he asked. "Under your bed, no doubt."

"Yes," Bragantosova answered. "It is." And she led him to the bed, lifted the spread, and showed the lieutenant the gaping hole in the floor.

At the sight of the huge bomb, the lieutenant gasped, turned, and raced out the door to sound the alarm. The militia came and immediately evacuated two thousand people from the surrounding area. A bomb squad carefully exploded Bragantosova's five-hundred-pound bomb, and a few days later the grateful local authorities gave Bragantosova a choice apartment in one of the new buildings.

An article in a Russian news magazine that reported Bragantosova's story ended with this sentence: "This proves that the authorities should always pay attention to ordinary citizens."

This true story about the old Russian woman with a bomb under her bed says to me that we ordinary citizens, young and old, must never stop telling those in authority that the presence of nuclear weapons in our world is like a bomb under all our beds. Even if we are laughed at or ignored, as Bragantosova was, we ordinary people know the danger, and we must keep on insisting that those in authority rid the world of this terrible menace.

I felt so different from the Japanese boys and girls
who wanted to practice their English with me. They gave
me pink candy wrapped in rice paper.
I imagined the intricate origami shapes they had down
pat. With my hands at my sides,
I wondered about the origami they could make.

Next on our tour, we made
the trip to Hiroshima, where I saw a wax girl
with wax flesh dripping off her sides.
As I stood before the Memorial, I learned that children gave
strings of cranes—thousands—that hung down
from the sculpture, to the deceased. Like lilies, but paper.

These were the noble paper shapes Japanese children made!
Rain misted down. I thought of the dripping girl.
My mother gave me her hand, I trembled inside.

kami = paper
takuan = a yellow pickle made from Japanese radish
koi = carp

Ꭷ Dead and Gone

by Marie G. Lee

Chess, my grandson, seems to think I know everything, so he asks me why there are no frogs in Lake Wichigrin.

I knew he was going to ask me that one day. My grandson notices everything. I have an answer prepared, though it's not the whole truth:

"There used to be frogs here when I was a little girl," I say, and I try to sound more like a know-it-all than like a sad person. "But things change. You know, global warming and the thinning of the ozone layer and all that."

Chess is twelve and a science whiz. This explanation seems to satisfy him. I mentally breathe a sigh of relief.

That night when the sun goes down, it settles like a glowing red pea, right on the lake. It reminds me so much—even though I don't want it to—of those nights long ago when my friends and I used to play War.

My parents brought me up to Lake Wichigrin for summers when I was a little girl. Back then there were only three cabins on our side of the lake; now there are at least ten. Ours was just a one-room box with an outhouse. Now our cabin has five rooms and running water. The old wood stove still has its place of honor in the middle of the cabin, but nowadays we do most of the cooking on an electric range.

It's nice to have all these conveniences in the cabin, but I do miss the sound of the frogs. I used to lie awake at night, listening to the soft bump-bump of the boat against the dock and the frogs croaking. The sounds said to me, summer, summer, summer. It's still pretty-sounding here, with the water and the occasional call of a loon. But I sure do miss those frogs.

The War started over who got Loon Point, the best part of the lake. The Point had many high-branched trees, perfect for attaching a rope so you could swing, Tarzanlike, into the water. And the trees' green leaves cast cool shadows, even during the hottest days of August. Loon Point also had a big rock shaped just like a loon's head—it was perfect for sunning and diving.

Bruce Weinstock

Nowadays, I hate this memory so much because the obvious question is, why didn't we just share Loon Point? Of course we should have shared. It would probably have been fun, all those kids playing together at the Point.

But that wasn't the way it was. We on our side of the lake believed we deserved exclusive rights to the Point—and the other-side kids disagreed. So we devoted all our time to proving our case: Loon Point was ours, and we'd fight for it if necessary.

From the three cabins there were me and my brother John, the Candella twins, and Tanya Foster and her cousin Jon. The other side of the lake was more spread out, so from a wider area came Todd and Max, Georgina, Jamie, and the huge Joey. We were pretty even.

Every summer, John and I were excited to see the our-side kids. When we got there, we made bonfires and roasted marshmallows and had a grand old time talking about what had happened during the school year. Our parents would go to bed, and we'd stay up next to the glow of the fire and start talking serious.

"Are they here yet? Have they been up to the Point?"

We never went up to the Point, except together. Sometimes the first kids to arrive went up to spy to see what was up, but neither side would show up until everything was "official."

The beginning part of the summer was most important. When we were good and ready, we would pack some soda, towels, and swim suits and head up there and make a lot of noise, basically waiting for the other-side kids. When they got there, we would tell them to leave, but of course they wouldn't.

We hated those other-side kids. I can't tell you exactly why. They were just kids, like us. But maybe it was because we thought of them as the other side, against us, so just looking at them would send my blood to boiling. Who did they think they were, anyway?

Once War was officially declared, anything could happen. We did things like dump the other-side kids' clothes into the water, steal their food. One day, one of the other-side boys punched my brother John right in the face, so we all rushed in there—even me! We were so mad that no matter how hard they hit, we hit even harder. I got my hair pulled and a big bruise on my arm, but I didn't feel anything—I just wanted to drive them out. And we did. Loon Point was ours for that summer.

Every summer we had to fight for it, though, and sometimes we lost and had to spend a whole summer somewhere else! That, of course, made us want to fight harder next time.

As we got older, the fighting got meaner. We were the first to use weapons—rocks. I actually didn't want to. I saw a movie once about some kids who stood on a bridge over a highway and dumped rocks over the side. The big rocks crashed into a car with a man, his wife, and a little baby. The little baby was on the momma's lap, and he died when the car crashed. I didn't want that to happen, even though there are no bridges on the roads that lead up to the lake.

But everyone else thought rocks would be a splendid idea, so we spent our days collecting them. The night when we met for War (we had started skirmishing at night . . . it was easier to fight when you couldn't see what the person looked like), I threw a rock and I heard it hit something, and someone said "Ow!" I remember feeling very proud of myself for that.

It's kind of strange how all my memories of the beautiful summers here at the lake are somehow attached to War. But I can't unattach them, because that's how my summers really happened.

There was that one summer when both sides decided to use frogs. Frogs didn't hurt as much as rocks, but if you were slapped in the face with one, they were cold and slimy.

In order to win the War, we figured we just had to get more frogs than the other side. Once the other side was "frogged" enough, they'd surrender.

We spent days collecting frogs, and we kept them in one of those ten-gallon containers that you use for keeping minnows. We kept it tethered at the dock and whenever someone caught a frog, he just threw it in the little door. After a while, though, it got so crowded that some of the frogs drowned. But we didn't mind too much because dead frogs are almost as good weapons as live ones.

And that night the sun set like a glowing red pea on the lake, just as it's doing tonight. It took three of us to lug that huge can of smelly frogs up to the Point. The other side was there, they threw the first bomb.

Splat! The frog hit me full in the face and left my cheek feeling slimy. It made me so mad I grabbed a bunch of frogs from the container and threw them with all my might. The fight was on. Frogs were flying everywhere—in the water, hitting trees, hitting faces.

The other side had a lot of frogs, but we had more. We kept throwing and throwing, and finally, there was a small voice that said, "We give up."

We were so happy that night. We envisioned all the great times we were going to have at Loon Point this summer. Swimming, sunning, playing.

The next day it rained, so we stayed in. The day after that it rained, too. And the day after. We got sick of playing Parcheesi and reading comic books, so we decided to go out to Loon Point in the rain just to look at it, what we'd won.

In our galoshes and rain gear, we trekked out there. We couldn't believe what we saw! There were dead frogs all over the place. Some were lying around with their insides hanging out, some had broken backs. A couple of them had their mouths open—I'd never seen a frog with its mouth open before. Even in the water, there were frogs floating, rain falling on them. On the rock there were dead soggy frogs with red blood on them. For some reason I thought frogs would have green blood, not red blood like ours.

In time, the weather cleared up and we went back and cleaned up. We threw the frog carcasses in the water, or into the woods. Sometimes now I wish we had buried them, or something.

I always wonder if the other frogs saw what happened to their brothers and decided to leave Lake Wichigrin. If you saw this happening to your brothers and sisters and friends, you probably wouldn't want to stay around either. In my imagination, those frogs packed up their bags and made the long march to another lake, Sand Lake, maybe.

Can you believe me? Such an old lady, yet I think so much about those frogs. I guess what bothers me the most is that the frogs were innocent creatures and we made them suffer so we could play War, which was not a very nice game in the first place.

I notice that Chess sometimes stays out late, playing with the other kids. I wonder if he ever plays games like War. I would like to think not, he's too sweet a kid. On the other hand, I was pretty sweet, too, with all my ribbons and lace, but I remember how it felt to throw that frog. I was fighting for something I believed in—not necessarily for Loon Point, but more for us as a group, our honor or something. Of course I see now how foolish it was—when it's too late.

"Chess," I say. He is putting his trunks in a towel. "I want to tell you something about the frogs."

"Not now, Grandma," he says. "I have to meet Steve and Bob."

"Okay," I say. "But remind me. I'll tell you why there aren't any frogs here at this lake."

Chess looks at me, cocks his head as he does when he's a little confused. But then he grabs his towel and runs out the door.

"Remind me to tell you!" I call after him.

"I will," he says. His white form fades away in the dark.

I sit and listen. The swish swish of the lake against the dock. A mosquito buzzes in my ear.

ᔑ The Forest

by Hushang Moradi Kermani
Translated from the Persian by Noucine Ansari

The water barrel stood in front of the shelter. From time to time a drop of water fell from the tap. The hot, dry earth sucked the water. The sun was shining in the sky, its heat burning the plain. The shelter was behind the first trench.

A sparrow flew over, sat on the barrel, and started to sing.

There had been no attack for twenty days. The soldiers on both sides were waiting for the attack to start any minute. The silence was bitter and frightening.

The soldier looked at the sparrow and said, "My daily guest is here." He took his glass of tea and went to sit by the barrel. He said to the sparrow, "What is happening over there?" Pointing to the enemy front he added, "Are you our spy, or their spy?"

The sparrow, perched on the tap, bent his head to get some water.

A soldier cried loudly from inside the shelter, "He is a double agent. The water is from here, the seeds are from there."

The soldier said, "He is lucky he doesn't know the meaning of war."

The other soldier commented, "How do you know he doesn't understand?"

The sparrow flew off. The soldier followed the bird with his eyes and looked and looked and looked until there was no trace. The soldier could see only the forms of date palms on the other side. He imagined the sparrow perched on an enemy palm, pecking at a ripe date.

The sergeant called out and said, "What is this? You are in the *forest* again? How many times do I have to tell you not to go there because it is in enemy sight?"

The soldier, sipping his tea from the glass, replied, "I cannot help it. I belong to the forest and I want to die there. The forest is thick. The branches and the leaves of the trees are so tangled together that you cannot even see the sky.

When I was a child I went to the forest with my father. He was a forester."

Another soldier said, "What's wrong with you? You are mad. You will get killed with the first bullet that falls in front of you. And there you are taking walks in your *forest*."

The solider bent down and put aside the mud and the pebbles surrounding the *forest*. Two tiny, thin, green leaves had sprung out from the bosom of the humid earth. The drop of water from the barrel watered the newly born plant.

A few days before, when the soldier was washing his face, he had noticed the plant near the spot of the water drops. The plant had started to grow. The soldier showed the seedling to his friends.

"Look here, boys! A forest!"

"Of course not. It's not a forest, it's a park!"

"What do you think it is?"

"Bean."

"Rice."

"Lentil."

"Barley."

Everyone said something.

"I wonder how this seed found its way to this desert, where even bushes of thorn are afraid to grow."

"This is life. It can be anywhere. It is 'friendship and love' that grows everywhere."

"Again the poet! You should read fewer books."

"Maybe the sparrow has brought the seed from the enemy front."

"Whatever you may think, from now on this is called the *forest*." The soldier had the final say.

Every afternoon, the soldiers sat by the shelter around the newly born plant, and they enjoyed it while drinking tea and talking together.

࿐

The soldier daydreamed about the forest of his childhood. In his memories he passed through tall grass and wildflowers. He walked under trees and beside bushes, and touched the soft humid moss on the tree trunks. He heard singing birds and picked a basket of wild figs for his mother. His father stayed inside the watch-hut. It was his father's job to be careful that no one cut the trees. Then the soldier had been eight and now he was sixteen.

჻

The sun was setting. A thin cloud was in the sky. The rays of the sun shone through the cloud. The cloud was red as though it was on fire.

That night, the soldiers left their shelters. Columns of men, old and young, stormed the enemy on foot. The enemy threw flares for its own forces. The flares cut through the darkness, filling the plain with light. The columns of men spread all over the plain. In front of them was the enemy and over their heads shells and fire. The explosions of the artillery shells and mines and the continuous sound of automatic rifles, mingled with human cries and the roar of airplanes, created an overwhelming music. The smell of gunpowder, mud, and burnt flesh and bones filled the air.

Rafal Olbinski

The soldiers retreated. Some who didn't want to retreat were still resisting. It was already dawn, light was spreading over the plain. The sound of the artillery shells was unending. The shells plowed the plain and tore the earth to pieces, and wounded soldiers rolled in blood and mud.

The soldier passed the shelter as he was retreating. He saw the barrel, full of holes, thrown into a corner. He rushed to his *forest*. It was hidden under heaps of earth. A shell hit the ground and exploded just beside the soldier. He threw himself on the ground. The burning fragment of a shell sat on his upper leg. He cried out, rolled with pain, and fell by his *forest*. Two soldiers lifted him by the armpits and carried him away.

ᢒ

The soldier was pacing the hospital yard with crutches. The gardener was watering the flowerpots.

The soldier's parents had come to take him home.

The sparrow came over from the other side, flying over the burned palms until it reached the plain. It passed the torn and bloody land, the ruined shelters, the boots, the clothes, and the remaining war equipment to sit on the barrel. There was no soldier and there was no water. The sparrow chirped. It looked to the ground and saw the *forest*. Its roots had gone deep into the earth, sucking what was left of the water. A tiny wheat plant with a small head of grain. The head was bent to the earth, thirsty and lonely. It was asleep, dreaming the nightmare of the war, trembling and fearful. The sparrow sat by the wheat plant, pecked at it, and woke it up. There was no war. The sparrow ate a seed from the wheat. The wind was blowing, it was soft and cool. The sky was clouded with clouds of rain.

The thirsty *forest* bent from side to side under the rain, as though it was dancing.

The sparrow crossed the barbed wires, passed to the other side of the frontier, and perched on a date palm.

ᔧ White Buffalo Calf Woman
and The Lakota Pipe Ceremony

Retold by Virginia Driving Hawk Sneve

Two hunters were hunting on the plains when they were suddenly blinded by a bright light. They cowered in fear, but the light faded and the hunters saw a beautiful young woman in white buckskin standing before them.

"Don't be afraid," the woman said, and smiled. "Go to your village and tell your people to prepare a council teepee. Soon I will come to them."

Back at the village, the people hurried to erect the great council teepee. They waited all night, but it wasn't until the sun rose that the woman came walking in its golden rays. In her hands she bore a bundle. She held it out to the people and walked into the teepee. The people followed.

The woman stood in the center and opened the bundle. "This is the sacred pipe. With it you and all of the people not yet born will send messages to the Great Spirit."

She held the pipe out to the people as she turned in the center of the teepee. "With this pipe walk upon the Earth. The Earth is your mother and she is sacred. With the pipe all people and creatures on the Earth will be joined with the four directions, and with the Great Spirit."

Next the woman taught them how to use the pipe in seven sacred rites. Then she gave the pipe to the chief. "Remember," she told him, "always to give the pipe respect and honor. Wherever the pipe is, let there be only peace and harmony."

She turned within the circle of the people and left the lodge, walking toward the east. As she went her white buckskin dress seemed to glow in the sun, and she turned into a white buffalo calf.

ᔧ

Following on the next page are the words of The Lakota Pipe Ceremony.

Amy Córdova

Turn to the east.

"Red is the east.

Where the daybreak star

of knowledge appears.

Red is the rising sun that brings us a new day."

Turn to the south.

"Yellow is the south.

Earth, our mother, gives the

bounty of summer with the warm wind."

Turn to the west.

"Black is the color of the west.

Where the sun sets. Black is

darkness and protects the spirits.

In the dark the spirits come to us."

Turn to the north.

"North is white.

Strength, purity, truth,

and endurance are of the north.

North covers Mother Earth with

the white blanket of cleansing snow."

Look to the sky.

"Father Sky gives life from the sun.

Father Sky gives the fire that

warms our teepees and the

life that moves our bodies."

Look to the earth.

"Green is the color for Mother Earth.

She gives us our food. We all start as tiny seeds.

We have grown through what she has given."

Turn to the center.

"Great Spirit, Creator of us all,

Creator of the four directions,

Creator of Mother Earth and Father Sky

and all related things. We offer this pipe."

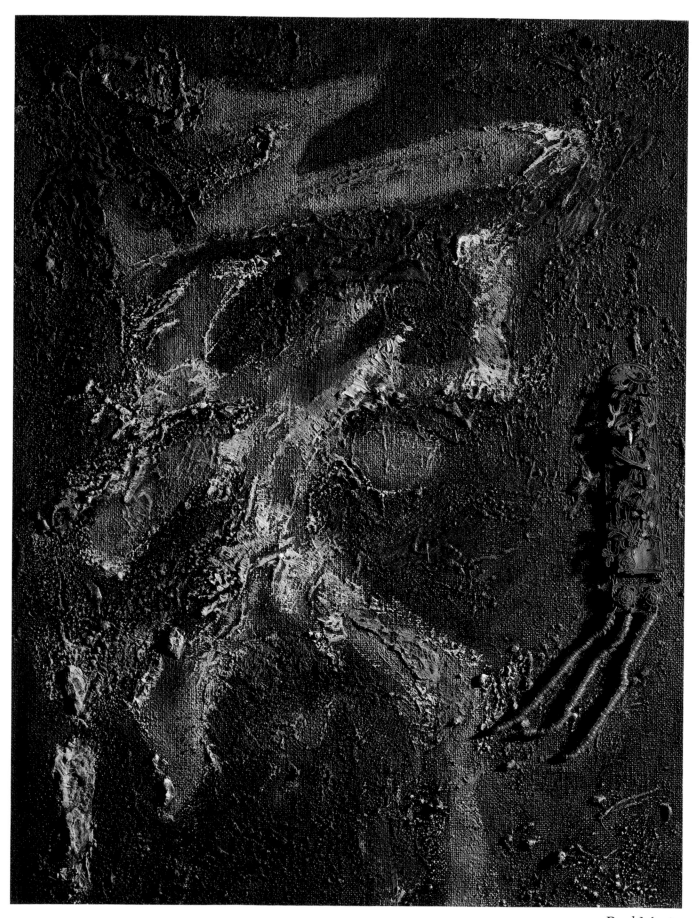

Paul Morin

ᔓ Never Again War!

by Yoko Kawashima Watkins

Though I am Japanese, I grew up in Nanam, North Korea, where winter came early and spring came slowly. Our house stood by a tall and graceful bamboo grove, where I played as a child.

The year was 1945, and near the end of July, Father was away in Manchuria. My brother, Hideyo, had just left to work in an ammunition factory. Almost without warning, my mother, my sister Ko, and I were forced to flee from the peaceful town. I was eleven and a half.

We made our way through the dangerous North Korean war zone and suffered terribly from hunger, thirst, and extreme heat beneath the sun. There was an air attack and a bomb fell near us and exploded. I fainted. Awakened from unconsciousness, I was frightened by a silent world. Mother's and Ko's lips were moving frantically. Mother's tears were dripping on my face and Ko was pressing my chest to stop the bleeding. All the way to Seoul I whined for my aching body and my deafness.

"Gosh! Whiny sister! Can't you shut up for a change?" Ko was disgusted after many days of listening to my complaints.

"I hurt! You'd cry too, if you got hurt."

"I would not!" Ko snapped. "You have done nothing but whine and fuss. This journey would be easier if you had been killed!"

I stopped walking and stared at her, dumbfounded. My sister wishing me dead!

"Ko! Don't you ever talk like that again!" Mother said. "Do you understand me? Never!"

At last we reached Seoul. Then we learned that powerful bombs had been dropped on Hiroshima and Nagasaki, and that Japan had surrendered. The Communists took over North Korea and we could not go back to our home in Nanam anymore. We became refugees and returned to Japan.

ᔓ

Mother, Ko, and I were able to get on a train from Fukuoka in 1945. The train headed to Tokyo. I was shocked to see how small the Japanese train was. It was packed with refugees and discharged soldiers. The aisles were filled with standees, and young men hung from the sides of the cars. On top of the train people clung together like grapes on the vine.

The train smelled of rotten fish. Ko said that many people would get off as the train stopped at the stations, and we would eventually find space to sit. I was hungry and thirsty, and the wound on my chest ached.

The train jolted along. Instead of many people getting off the train, more got on and we were pushed and squeezed. Again and again my chest ached and I put my hand over the sore spot to protect it. Ko leaned against the wooden panel of a toilet, Mother leaned against Ko, and I leaned on Mother. I thought my legs had turned to a pair of sticks and that I could not stand much more.

When the train pulled into the Hiroshima station everybody got off and went to the toilet right on the platform. I was moved with a great sense of relief. I went to the toilet also for I did not know just when the train would stop again.

The platform was filled with people suffering from radiation sickness. Some, sitting down and panting, begging for water; some staggering, not knowing where they were going, spitting black bloodlike liquids. The skin from their foreheads hung over severely damaged, popped-out eyes. From a man's burned head rusty-colored liquid was running over his face and neck, down his body. He was trying to wipe it away, then a whole side of his facial skin peeled off, his hands and arms equally burned and his flesh covered with maggots.

A girl my age was shrieking, maybe looking for her mother or someone else she knew. The skin of her arm was hanging from her wrist, flipping-flapping on the ground.

A woman's face was cut to pieces; what she had on was shredded, her hair burned down to the root, and, with damaged eyes, she was examining almost decayed small bodies to search for her little one.

I could see the destroyed city from where I stood. For so long I had complained about my aches, the deafness, the hunger and thirst, but I stopped. I looked at Mother and Ko and realized there were others who were in worse condition than I. How fortunate I was to have my family.

Four decades after the atomic bomb was dropped on Hiroshima, I had a chance to visit the city again. It is now beautifully rebuilt. Once it was feared that nothing would grow on radiated land; now the trees and flowers are thriving, and hundreds of doves joyfully greet visitors. With all the rebuilding, the skeleton of one building has been left as a reminder of the tragic day of August 6.

I went to the museum in the Peace Park. As I walked past the wartime items my head was like a revolving lantern of scenes of the horrible bygone days. I could not breathe. I went outside to sit on a bench. Families of the bombing victims were participating in a ceremony. They were commemorating the fortieth anniversary of the dropping of the first atomic bomb.

Not too far from where I sat, a man was feeding doves. I could not tell his age because of his keloid-scarred face and hands. When the feeding bag was empty he slowly stood, his body almost bent in half. He looked upward, circling his head and body to the cloudless sky, and dragged himself to where the Peace Bell hung, near Sadako's statue. The bell was made in memory of the victims and for world peace.

The man managed to climb four shallow steps. He stretched his bent body to the best of his ability to reach the loglike bell striker. With all his might he tolled the bell. The deep serene sound mingled with the sutras chanted by the participants and echoed into the Hiroshima sky, as if to tell the world, "Never Again War!"

ᔊ My Land

by Rigoberta Menchú Tum
Translated from the Spanish by Elizabeth Abello

Mother earth, mother country
The bones and memories of my ancestors
Lie here
Within you are buried
Grandparents, grandchildren, and children.

Bones upon bones of your people
Are piled here
The bones of this land's beautiful children
146 fertilized the corn, the yucca
Malanga, the chilacayotes
The pumpkins, the guicoyes, and the guisquilas.

My own bones were formed here.
My umbilicus was buried here
And thus I stayed here
Year after year
Generation after generation.

Land of mine, land of my grandparents
Your scattered rains,
Your clear rivers,
Your free air that caresses,
Your green mountains
And the burning heat of your sun
Made the sacred corns grow and multiply
And formed the bones of this grandchild.

Land of mine, mother of my grandparents,
I wish I could caress your beauty
Contemplate your serenity
And accompany your silence
I wish I could ease your pain
Cry your tears which fall
From seeing your children
Scattered all over the world
Begging shelter in faraway lands
Without happiness, without peace
Without homeland, with nothing.

Paul Morin

I sit with my watercolors on a high mountain meadow,
marveling at the simple beauty I see before me.
Surely such a sight has the power to give us a sense of peace.

Nature provides the gift of inner peace.
We have only to stop, look, and listen, and the gift will be ours.
—Wendell Minor

﹏ From The Song of the Plaza

by Ana Maria Machado
Translated from the Portuguese by Julie Kline

First, it's good to say the time in which these things come to pass.

It is the present. But a stretched-out present, I don't know exactly what year. Some point between the time when the mothers and the grandmothers were children and the time in which the great-grandchildren are going to be born. Between the time when the first atomic bombs began to plant their mortal mushroom venom on the face of the earth, and the time in which the International Circus Festival will be the last celebratory competition that will remain—after the Great Kingdom of the West and the Great Empire of the East have already ended the Great Sports Games upon resolving that, if one had to go play in the other's territory, they would play no more. A time in which there will be yet more madmen without sense in charge of the great powers, and every government will be making more bombs, more missiles, more death rays. Always with the same old talk that it is necessary to have terrible weapons to guarantee peace. Always playing at starting small little wars in the countries of others who had nothing to do with it, just to show that the great kingdoms and empires can test their armies and show their force.

So it's at that time that we leave the Other and return to the Real. Time to revive, to stop War, to guarantee Peace.

Having explained the time, we still need to explain the place. We have returned to the song of the plaza. Only now it is no longer the little plaza of a small town, with a fountain in front of the church. It is a big modern city, full of people, of automobiles, of movement.

From the place I am, dressed as a clown and calling for the spectacle, I see my three friends in the middle of the crowd. Asiul, Leafar, and Ocram, having already left the other side, and named Luisa, Rafael, and Marco, but eternally Columbine, Harlequin, and Pierrot. They buy balloons, eat ice cream, stop in front of a religious preacher who, upon finishing singing some hymns, begins his sermon.

Jessica Krause

From where I am, I can't hear what he says very well, but some pieces of sentences are clear:

"Watch and pray because the hour is at hand . . . and the four horsemen will come—War, Hunger, Pestilence, and Death—and there will be calls and cries, and fire and blood . . . and the seven angels will play their trumpets. . . ."

There was no way to hear any better, but I perceived that by his language the preacher was also very worried by the climate of war that threatened all of us. And whoever stops there at the newsstand on the corner will see that the headlines say the same. The language of the newspapers is another, different from the preacher's words. Or mine. But in the end, it's all the same story.

There is always a side that says "Mine!" And another that responds, "No, it's mine!" and craziness spreads.

Always the talk that it's necessary to have a terrible weapon—now the atomic bomb, or a total nuclear armament—in order to guarantee peace.

Always each one thinking that people can only be one thing or another, harlequins or pierrots, westerners or easterners, black-and-white or colors.

Now it is talk full of solemn or abstract words: Justice, Liberty. One side saying it is owner of all the world's liberty, that outside its kingdom only slavery exists. The other saying that its territory is the only one that is just, that beyond is only exploitation.

No one recognizes what the navigators already knew, that the earth is round, that here is already there, that it is possible to arrive in the East by traveling through the West. That the beginning is the end. It seems no one sees that between day and night there are twilight and the dawn, that someone can want to be just and free at the same time, pierrot and harlequin, black-and-white and colors, mestizo like Rafael and Marco, very mestizo like Luisa.

The shouts of the crowd, finding their way, turn into a song.

Suddenly everyone is singing a new song, the song of the plaza, the true magical words of transformation:

"Long live the Dove of Peace! War nevermore!"

At that moment the girl Luisa, Dove-Columbine, transformed into a little white dove, flies upward.

She flies as if in a ballet, to the sound of the crowd's song in the plaza, a song giving her new life.

Before reaching the vastness of the sky, she soars above the audience, blessing the song of the plaza, blessing everything and everyone, as the first dove of peace should have done centuries and centuries ago, the one that brought Noah an olive branch while God blessed mankind with the first rainbow in history.

And speaking of rainbows, there he is, Harlequin, forever playing at appearing and disappearing in the sky, between the rain and the sun, joining opposites, with his clothing of colored rags.

With a rapid gesture, I free a white balloon that was caught in the canvas of the tent roof, and it begins to rise. Balloon? The moon, of course! Seeking his place in the darkening sky, shy Pierrot goes seeking the threads of clouds that hide him until everyone sleeps and he can appear without care, clarity illuminating the darkness, caressing Columbine asleep in the towers of churches and palaces in all the songs of all the plazas in the world.

Commenting on the marvels of the day at the circus, the audience shortly returns home and the plaza empties.

Only my solitary figure remains.

I think about the power of change that the song of the plaza can have when the crowd raises its voice.

And I give to all of you an account of what happened, speaking, inventing, using the only weapon that I have against war and against the other horsemen announced by the angels' trumpets and the newspaper headlines. A limited weapon, I recognize, but full of cleverness. The only one that can be a companion to Dove-Columbine, Dove of Peace, because it is the only one that serves to call people, to reunite opposites, to summon forces, to overcome limits.

I really only know that.

I play with illusion, I make magic and buffoonery, I am jester of the opposite and the real, balancer of fantasy, puppeteer of characters, juggler of words, creator of tales and of stories. I do what I think. Each one who comes to the plaza and does the same counts as one. The spectacle of life has to continue.

⮵ Come Back, Palestine, Come Back

by Omar S. Castañeda
Retold from a story by Rima Hassouneh

Rima and Dima were nearly doubled over when Baba reached to take their hands in his. They had been gazing excitedly at the shells and scattered bones washed up on the beach. Baba twirled them by the Arabian Gulf and they felt suddenly whisked into the safety of their father. Where they now lived, the beach was a boisterous white of countless shells ground to sand by the rolling waves of the Kuwaiti shore. The island of Faylakah seemed to bob like a turtle in the water, with the peaks of the Iranian mountains combing the sky beyond the fuming oil fields to the south.

"Now play with your sister," Baba told them. His arms were tired. "I have to go back to work." Baba eyed them warningly. "And don't tease her so much."

Behind them, small flowers spotted the sparse and tawny grasses of the dunes. All around, the air smelled of burst shells, of sea wind and salt life, as spindrift spumed up and lifted off like a tattered koufiyyeh. A great flurrying and squabbling of gulls reminded the twins of their father's discussions in the kiosks with other men of Palestine. Their father was an important man, but that only made it harder for them to be in Kuwait after the Gulf War, when Palestinians wanted more than anything to have their own homeland.

They watched him go back up from shore to the office. On his way, he lifted his hand to point out the twins for Rana. Unlike her older sisters, Rana was too young to feel the same about Palestine. And perhaps because it seemed that they would never return to the West Bank, Rima and Dima began to feed Rana's questions with outlandish stories.

Once, Rana asked innocently, "Why do the clouds move?" She looked inland and watched the clouds pass beyond the tall building where Baba worked.

Rima winked at Dima. "It really isn't the clouds," she answered.

Laila Shawa

"The buildings are moving," Dima said.

"The buildings?" Rana clutched a patch of grass to steady herself should everything suddenly lurch into motion.

Rima grew serious. "The building is a ship."

"It goes sailing at night," Dima added.

"When we're all fast asleep."

Rana clutched the patch so hard a clump pulled free in her hand.

The twins continued. "It goes out past the Strait of Hormuz and to the Arabian Sea at night. Baba and the other men tie up the sails and pull up the anchor. They take it all the way to Palestine. They take messages to our families."

Rana shook her head. "The Israelis would never let that happen."

"It's a special ship," Rima said. "It takes them into Palestine without anyone stopping them or searching them. They aren't asked any questions. All they do is take messages to our families and give food and medicine. Then the ship comes back here in the morning before anyone wakes up."

Rana crossed her arms and stared at her older sisters. "I don't believe it!"

"Oh, it's true!" they answered. "The building rocks back and forth because the land floats on the ocean. Why do you think the water is so close?"

Rana watched the bulge and roll of the sea.

"To keep the building still," Dima said, "they bury the anchor during the day. Otherwise, it would sail away forever."

"And we would be here forever," Rima said.

Rana wanted more than anything to go find the secret place for the anchor, but the twins told her they couldn't. What if they made the building float away? What if they broke the chain? Where would they be then? What would Baba say?

And that was how the older twins and their sister Rana played.

One day, Baba came to them on the beach. He pulled the twins aside and told them the news. He would be going to the West Bank with other officials of Palestine.

"What does it mean?" the twins asked.

"Perhaps nothing," he said. "Perhaps something good for our people. It seems that maybe there's a little bit of hope for something now. A little bit for peace, perhaps." He stroked the hair of the girls, one head in each big hand. "We'll have to see what happens together, my sweeties."

Rana squirmed close for her share of affection. "Why can't we go with you?"

Baba swooped her up in one great motion and spun on his heels. Rana squealed. "Don't worry," he told her. "When you want me to come home, just say, 'Come back, Baba, come back,' and I'll be back before you know it."

The family had a big lunch for Baba that afternoon. They ate msakhan and yoghurt, and Mama made baklawa for dessert. Other Palestinians were celebrating too. Later the evening filled with the music of the oud, tableh, and qanun.

The next day, Baba left and the twins took Rana to the beach. They watched the sea and birds in silence. Finally Rana asked, "Why do the waves come in like that?"

"Because someone is always calling them," Dima said.

Rima wiggled her fingers across the sand. "You can call it too. Just like when you want to call for Baba."

Rana perked up. "How?"

"Go ahead," they said, "tell it to come. Say 'Come here, sweetie. Come here.' You'll see what happens."

So Rana did. She crept close to the waves, just far enough away so her shoes stayed dry, and spoke to the great Arabian Gulf.

"Come here, sweetie," she said. "Come here."

The waves rolled in. They tumbled over the beach, hissing as they broke, and chased Rana back to her sisters.

The three laughed giddily.

"Come here, sweetie," Rima said.

"Come here, sweetie," Dima said.

"Sweetie," Rana shouted, arms outstretched before the wide gulf, "please come here."

The sea tumbled and crashed for them. As far as they looked to the left and as far as they looked to the right, the sea tumbled for them. It somersaulted and splashed and sent white foam across the sand.

Several days later, a man brought a letter back from Baba. Mama called the

☙ Soldier Jim and the Bird of Peace

Written and illustrated by Niki Daly

Left-right, left-right, here comes Jim, looking for a war.
Left-right, left-right, **Attention!**

He's got his gun! He's got his orders!
On the left, quick **March!**

Left-right, left-right, **Halt!**

Here, at a crossroad on the way to war,
stands a devil with fear in his eye.
And this is what he says:
"Soldier Jim, carry me
and I'll show you the Road to War."

Up jumps the devil, and his name is **FEAR.**
On the left, quick **March!**

Left-right, left-right, **Halt!**
Here, at a crossroad on the way to war,
stands a devil with terror in his eyes.
And this is what he says:
"Soldier Jim, carry me
and I'll show you the Road to War."

Up jumps the devil and his name is **TERROR**.
On the left, quick **March!**
And a mighty dead weight it is
for Soldier Jim to carry.
Left . . . . right . . . . left . . . . right . . . . **Halt!**

Here, at a crossroad on the way to war,
stands a devil with death in his eyes.
And this is what he says:
"Soldier Jim, carry me
and I'll show you the Road to War."

Up jumps the devil, and his name is **DEATH**.
On the left, quick **March!**
And with every left,
the road gets longer.
And with every right,
the burden gets too hard to bear.
And oh! What stories of horror they tell!

Auschwitz, **Hiroshima,** **Vietnam.**

With a left . . . with a right . . . **MERCY!**
Here, at the last crossroad on the way to war,
sits the Bird of Peace, in the hand of Hope.

And this is what Jim shouts:

**"Away, you devils!
No more War! I'll lay down my gun!"**

Off charge Fear, Terror, and Death,
their war-cries and siren-screams
echoing down the Road to War.

All is calm now.
"Here," says Hope, carefully placing
the Bird of Peace in Jim's hand.
"Thank God," says Jim.

Amen.

৵ Children Hope for a Peaceful Future
by Camy Condon

In November 1989, a group of students at Arroyo del Oso Elementary School in Albuquerque, New Mexico, were involved in enrichment classes that were participating in the Future Problem Solving Competition, a nationwide program in which teams of students work together to solve a social problem scenario set in the near future. The November assignment was for students to brainstorm solutions to the arms race. One of the solutions generated by the children was the implementation of programs to educate future generations about peace. The children were inspired by the story of how the peace statue in memory of Sadako Sasaki at Hiroshima Peace Park was built by the children of Japan. The Albuquerque students decided to embark on the building of a monument that would express their hopes for a future in which no child need ever suffer the consequences of war.

With the help of their teachers, the students began raising funds from children all over the world, hoping to have enough money to build their statue by August 1995. They saw the fiftieth anniversary of the bombings of Hiroshima and Nagasaki as a fitting moment to draw attention to the need to educate about peaceful solutions to world problems. In five years of hard work, the children raised over $30,000, donated by 69,000 supporters from all fifty states and sixty-nine foreign countries.

In 1994, children were asked to submit drawings of what the peace monument should look like. More than 300,000 designs were submitted. A panel of seven judges, ages seven to sixteen, chose "A Peace Garden" by eighteen-year-old Noe Martinez as the winner. Martinez envisioned a garden that would be a "refreshing oasis in the desert of Los Alamos, New Mexico" with a globe as a focal point and "encircling beds of flowers that form the shape of the continents of the earth. The flowers are a perfect symbol of life, peace, and a new beginning." Los Alamos was to be its site because the city originated as a nuclear weapons lab city. The first atomic bomb was tested in the Alamogordo Desert near Los Alamos.

The winning entry for The Children's Peace Statue designed by Noe Martinez

The city of Los Alamos was, at first, pleased to receive "A Peace Garden." Adults representing some veterans' groups, though, objected to the monument. They convinced the Los Alamos city leaders that the children's efforts were unpatriotic and disrespectful of the men and women who fought in the Pacific in World War II. During the course of the debate about the placement of the garden, it became clear that the idea of peace is threatening to some adults. Dana Kaplan, fourteen years old, defended the monument, saying that its purpose is "the hope by children of today for a peaceful future. And that is all." Nonetheless, Los Alamos decided against accepting the monument.

The problem was resolved when the city of Albuquerque volunteered to place the monument at the Albuquerque Museum. The thirty-one days of ceremonies planned for its unveiling can take place in August 1995 as planned. Three thousand names of its supporters will be read each day.

Children around the world, spearheaded by a small group in one classroom, have made a powerful statement for world peace. Their work is not finished. The monument will need a fund to maintain it, and the expenses of constructing it are not fully paid. To become a Supporter of "A Peace Garden," checks can be made out to: NMCC, Peace Statue, or Albuquerque Community Foundation, Peace Statue, and mailed to Children's Peace Statue, P.O. Box 12888, Albuquerque, New Mexico 87195-2888.

WALK TOGETHER CHILDREN

O, Walk to-geth-er child-ren, Don't you get weary,
Sing to-geth-er child-ren, Don't you get weary,

Walk to-geth-er child-ren, Don't you get weary,
Sing to-geth-er child-ren, Don't you get weary,

Walk to-geth-er child-ren, Don't you get weary, There's a
Sing to-geth-er child-ren, Don't you get weary, There's a

great camp meet-ing in the Prom-ised Land.

Going to mourn and never tire, — Mourn and never

tire, —— Mourn and nev-er tire, —— There's a

great camp meet-ing in the Prom-ised Land. O,

123

Ashley Bryan

ᠵ How to Fold a Paper Crane

By George Levenson

The Paper ᠵ Origami paper comes in a variety of colors, sizes, and textures and is available in most art and stationery stores. Typically, it is thin, strong, and holds a crease well. It is usually colored or patterned on one side and plain on the other. To make a crane (and most other origami figures), the paper must be square. Almost any paper can be cut into squares and folded into beautiful paper birds. It's easy to make a perfect square out of a magazine page, gift wrap, or any sheet of paper with square corners. Lift the bottom corner of the sheet and fold it diagonally so the bottom edge meets the side edge of the paper. Cut off the strip of paper that remains at the top, and you have a perfect square! It's best to fold your first cranes with a piece of paper that is at least 5" square. Eventually you can make them very tiny.

Mastery ᠵ While the crane is one of the more advanced origami designs, it can be mastered by most nine-year-olds. Repetition is the key to memorizing all the steps, and the best results come from matching the corners and making the creases sharp. Don't be discouraged if your first few cranes look a little scrunched or lop-sided. After you get it right the first time, make five more within the next day, and the technique will stay with you for a long time. One of the best ways to remember the steps is to teach them to someone else.

Display ᠵ Once the cranes are finished, they can be strung together in garlands. Attach a string to a long needle, push it through the hole in the bottom of each crane, and bring it out through the point in the center of the crane's back. Be sure to tie a knot at the end of the string. To distinguish the cranes on the string, add a 1/4" piece of plastic straw or coffee stirrer between each crane.

More information ᠵ These written instructions accompany the live action video *How to Fold a Paper Crane*, designed for individual and group instruction. A whimsical pair of hands guided by a lively narrator clearly shows all 26 steps. For information call (800) 827-0949.

Begin with a square piece of paper — ideally one side colored and the other plain. Place the colored side face up on the table. In all diagrams, the shaded part represents the colored side.

1. Fold diagonally to form a tri-angle. Be sure the points line up. Make all creases very sharp. You can even use your thumbnail.

Unfold the paper. (important!)

2. Now fold the paper diagonally in the opposite direction, forming a new triangle.

Unfold the paper and turn it over so the white side is up. The dotted lines in the diagram are creases you have already made.

3. Fold the paper in half to the "east" to form a rectangle.

Unfold the paper.

4. Fold the paper in half to the "north" to form a new rectangle.

Unfold the rectangle, but don't flatten it out. Your paper will have the creases shown by the dotted lines in the figure on the right.

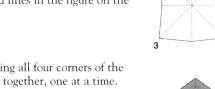
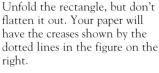

5. Bring all four corners of the paper together, one at a time. This will fold the paper into the flat square shown on the right. This square has an open end where all four corners of the paper come together. It also has two flaps on the right and two flaps on the left.

6. Lift the upper right flap, and fold in the direction of the arrow. Crease along line a-c.

7. Lift the upper left flap and fold in the direction of the arrow. Crease along the line a-b.

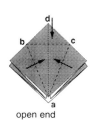

open end

8. Lift the paper at point d (in the previous diagram) and fold down the triangle bdc. Crease along the line b-c.

Undo the three folds you just made (steps 6, 7, and 8), and your paper will have the crease lines shown on the right.

9. Lift just the top layer of the paper at point a. Think of this as opening a frog's mouth. Open it up and back to line b-c. Crease the line b-c inside frog's mouth.

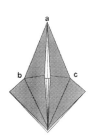

Press on points b and c to reverse the folds along lines a-b and a-c. The trick is to get the paper to lie flat in the long diamond shape shown on the right. At first it will seem impossible. Have patience.

10 to 13 Turn the paper over. Repeat Steps 6 to 9 on this side. When you have finished, your paper will look like the diamond below with two "legs" at the bottom.

14 & 15 Taper the diamond at its legs by folding the top layer of each side in the direction of the arrows along lines a-f and a-e so that they meet at the center line.

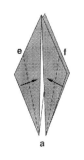

16 & 17 Flip the paper over. Repeat steps 14 and 15 on this side to complete the tapering of the two legs.

18. The figure on the right has two skinny legs. Lift the upper flap at point f (be sure it's just the upper flap), and fold it over in the direction of the arrow – as if turning the page of a book. This is called a "book fold".

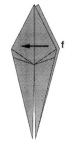

Flip the entire figure over.

19. Repeat this "book fold" (step 18) on this side. Be sure to fold over only the top "page".

20. The figure on the right looks like a fox with two pointy ears at the top and a pointy nose at the bottom. Open the upper layer of the fox's mouth at point a, and crease it along line g-h so that fox's nose touches the top of the fox's ears.

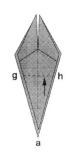

21. Turn the figure over. Repeat step 20 on this side so that all four points touch.

22. Now for another "book fold". Lift the top layer of the figure on the right (at point f), and fold it in the direction of the arrow.

23. Flip the entire figure over. Repeat the "book fold" (step 22) on this side.

24 & 25 There are two points, a and b, below the upper flap. Pull out each one, in the direction of the arrows, as far as the dotted lines. Press down along the base (at points x and y) to make them stay in place.

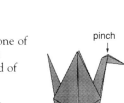

26. Take the end of one of the points, and bend it down to make the head of the crane. Using your thumbnail, reverse the crease in the head, and pinch it to form the beak. The other point becomes the tail.

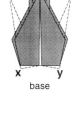

Open the body by blowing into the hole underneath the crane, and then gently pulling out the wings. And there it is!

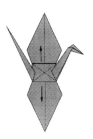

ᴈ About the Contributors

Marjorie Agosín, from Chile, is a widely published poet and human rights activist. Among her recent works: *Circle of Madness* and *A Cross and a Star: Memoirs of a Jewish Girl in Chile*. She writes: "Hiroshima and Nagasaki/Words to be spoken out loud/Words of places and faces that must be named/From the ashes of oblivion." *Photo credit: Ted Polobaum*

Tomie Arai is a Japanese-American visual artist. She is a recent recipient of a 1994 NEA Visual Artist Fellowship and a 1994 Joan Mitchell Grant. Her work is in the collections of the Museum of Modern Art, the Library of Congress, and the Washington State Arts Commission. She has two children, Masai and Akira, and lives in New York City.

The paintings and drawings of **Marshall Arisman** have been exhibited internationally. They can be seen in the collections of the Brooklyn Museum, the National Museum of American Art, and the Smithsonian. He created a book of paintings and drawings describing the emotional and spiritual impact of the nuclear war on society. His political drawings can be seen in the Op-Ed page of *The New York Times*, *The Nation*, and *Time*. Mr. Arisman is Chairman of an M.F.A. program at the School of Visual Arts in New York. *Photo credit: Karen Jill Marks*

Barbara Bedway won a Pushcart Prize for her short story about two children living in Beirut during Lebanon's civil war. Her essays and articles have appeared in *The New York Times*, *Child*, and *The American Voice*, among other publications.

Joseph Bruchac's poems, articles, and stories have appeared in over 500 publications. He has authored more than fifty books for adults and children, including *Thirteen Moons on a Turtle's Back*, a 1993 Notable Children's Book in the Language Arts and an IRA Young Adults' and Teachers' Choice. His fellowships and awards include the Hope S. Dean Award for Notable Achievement in Children's Literature and the 1993 Benjamin Franklin Award as "Person of the Year" from the Publishers' Marketing Association.

Born in 1923, **Ashley Bryan** grew up in the Bronx, New York. He earned a degree in philosophy at Columbia University, and illustrated his first children's book in 1967. Among his works are *The Ox of the Wonderful Horns*, an ALA Notable Children's Book, and *All Night, All Day*, a Coretta Scott King Honor Book. Mr. Bryan is Professor Emeritus of Art at Dartmouth University. *Photo credit: Matthew Wysocki*

Diana Bryan, a former pupeteer, teaches at the Parsons School of Design and has illustrated two children's videos, *The Fisherman and His Wife* and *The Monkey People*. She is currently working on thirteen murals for the New York Public Library's main branch for their centennial exhibit of the 100 Best Books of this century.

Among the books **Nancy Carpenter** has illustrated for children are: *Sitti's Secrets*, *Masai and I*, and *The Tree that Came to Stay*. She also contributes drawings regularly to *The New York Times Week-in-Review*. Ms. Carpenter lives in Hoboken, New Jersey.

Peter Catalanotto has illustrated several books for children, including *Who Came Down that Road?* and *Cecil's Story*. He wrote and illustrated *Dylan's Day Out*. Mr. Catalanotto grew up on Long Island and attended Pratt Institute in Brooklyn, New York.

Omar S. Castañeda was born in Guatemala and moved to the United States at the age of three. He is the author of *Cunuman* and *Among the Volcanoes* and over forty journal publications. Mr. Castañeda has won various grants and awards, including the 1993 Charles H. and N. Mildred Nilon Award for Excellence in Minority Fiction. *Photo credit: Bleu Castañeda*

One-man exhibitions of **Peter E. Clarke**'s work have been on view throughout the world, and he is represented in private and public collections including The National Gallery, South Africa and the Library of Congress, Washington D.C. His picture in *The Wings of Peace*, "Homage," is a linocut-print with watercolor paints. He chose the image inspired by the American poet Langston Hughes's words "because it is really a homage to the human spirit." Mr. Clarke lives in South Africa. *Photo credit: Claudia Cavanagh*

Camy Condon is the volunteer Adult Advisor to the six-year effort of building the 1995 Children's Peace Statue. She is Coordinator of Intergenerational Programs at the New Mexico Conference of Churches. She is also a mom, an author of ten books on crafts and culture in Japan, and a community puppeteer. She lives in Albuquerque, New Mexico, with her husband and five geese.

The works of **Amy Córdova** have been exhibited in solo and group shows and corporate and private collections. She received an NEA Visual Arts Fellowship and a COMPAS grant for a project honoring the women of Central America. She has also illustratrated a picture book. Ms. Córdova resides in the Minneapolis-St. Paul area.

Niki Daly won a Parents Choice award and the South African Katrine Harries Award for *Not So Fast, Songololo*, one of his many books for children. He lives in Mowbray, Cape Town, with his wife, Jude Daly, and their two sons, Joseph and Leo.

Edwidge Danticat was born in Haiti in 1969. She moved to the United States when she was twelve. She is a graduate of Barnard College and Brown University's M.F.A. program. Her first novel, *Breath, Eyes, Memory*, and her collection of short stories *Krik Krak* were published in the spring of 1994. She lives in Brooklyn, New York. *Photo credit: Len Irish*

Robert Del Tredici has been documenting the nuclear age in words and pictures since 1978. He has covered commercial and nuclear power, uranium mining, nuclear weapons production, Hiroshima and Nagasaki, the Russian nuclear weapons complex, and the cleanup of the U.S. H-bomb factory system. He teaches photography and lives in Montreal with his wife, Setsumi, and their five-year-old son, Felix. *Photo credit: Yoshito Matsushige*

Leo and Diane Dillon married in 1957 and joined forces to become one artist, both working on the same piece of art. They have taught at the School of Visual Arts in New York, and have illustrated book jackets, album covers, posters, and magazine articles. In the 1980s, they began to focus on textbook art, picture books, and jacket art, and have received numerous awards for their work including two Caldecott medals for *Ashanti to Zulu* and *Why Mosquitoes Buzz in People's Ears*, the Hugo, the

Hamilton King Award, and a Gold Medal for Children's Book Illustration from the Society of Illustrators.

Jean Durandisse was born in Leogane, Haiti. His work has been featured in several books and prints, among them *Haiti: Voodoo Kingdom to Modern Riviera*. Last spring, he was given an award of Excellence in All Categories by Le Cercle des Artistes du Quebec for his painting "La Danse Vodou." Mr. Durandisse currently resides in Montreal, Canada, where he has taught high school for the past twenty years.

Tom Feelings has illustrated over twenty books and received the School of Visual Arts' Outstanding Achievement Award, eight Certificates of Merit from The Society of Illustrators, an NEA Visual Artists Fellowship, two Coretta Scott King Awards and two Caldecott Honor Medals for *Moja Means One* and *Jambo Means Hello*. He is an art professor at the University of South Carolina in Columbia.

Shinya Fukatsu was born in 1957 in the Aichi prefecture of Japan. He graduated from Chuo Art School in Tokyo, Japan, and has won various awards, including the Prize of the Nippon Graphic Exhibition. In 1990, he held a one-person exhibition at the Tokyo American Club in the Genkan Gallery, Japan.

Nikki Grimes is the author of many books for children including *Something on My Mind*, an ALA Notable Book which also won a Coretta Scott King Award. In addition to her work for children, Ms. Grimes frequently writes articles for women's magazines, and is the author of a work of historical fiction for adults. *Photo credit: Joelle Petit Adkins*

Bent Haller was born in 1946 in Denmark. He has been educated in the fine arts, and his literary debut was in 1976. Mr. Haller writes for children and adults and works for television, radio, theater, and film.

Sheila Hamanaka is an award-winning fine artist who has been illustrating children's books for the past seven years. She is best known as the author/illustrator of *The Journey*, based on a five-panel mural she painted about the history of Japanese people in America. The book focuses on the Japanese internment camps of World War II. She also wrote and illustrated *All the Colors of the Earth*, *Peace Crane*, and the forthcoming *Be-Bop-A-Do-Walk*.

Paul Hunt grew up in an industrial part of South Wales, United Kingdom. He studied illustration in Wiltshire, England, graduating in the late 1980s. His first picture book, *Night Diary*, was runner-up in the Mother Goose Awards, 1993. Other books include *Dave and the Toothfairy* and Hans Christian Andersen's *The Red Shoes*. Mr. Hunt has illustrated many book jackets as well. He lives in London, England.

Murv Jacob is a painter and pipemaker of Kentucky Cherokee descent. He has won numerous awards for his work, including the Grand Award at the Trail of Tears Art Show, and has illustrated over twenty-five books. Mr. Jacob lives in Tahlequah, Oklahoma, capital of the Cherokee Nation.

Michio Kaku is professor of nuclear physics at the City University of New York. He graduated from Harvard University (summa cum laude) in 1968 and received his Ph.D. from the University of California at Berkeley in 1972. He has authored eight books and seventy scientific articles, and is on the National Advisory Board of Peace Action. In 1982, he spoke before a million people in Central Park, New York, at the largest peace rally in the history of America. Dr. Kaku hosts a weekly radio program on WBAI-FM and can be heard on sixty radio stations around the country on Pacifica Network News.

Miya Kanzaki has written a book review for *Parnassus: Poetry in Review*, has published poems and articles in journals and newspapers, and is a graduate of the Columbia University MFA Writing Program. She remembers, vividly, how moved she was when she visited Hiroshima as a child. She always wants to hold on to that feeling because it reminds her to be grateful for peace. She lives in New York City.

Hushang Moradi Kermani was born in 1944 in a village near the Iranian city of Kerman. He has won various national prizes, and in 1992 was chosen as distinguished author by the Hans Christian Andersen jury. His works include *The Story of That Cask* and *The Stories of Magid*.

"Whenever I think of Hiroshima, I hear the frightened cry of a little girl, gripping at the air and screaming 'WHY?'"

Jessica Krause lives in New York City. She is a set designer for music videos and theater, and teaches art to children. In the past, she has worked in documentary film and advertising. She paints portraits and landscapes, creating three-dimensional pieces inspired by her set designs. She works in acrylic, watercolor, pencil, wood, and clay.

Setsu Kunii graduated from Tama Bijutsu University in Japan, and now works as a designer. Her art has been exhibited in galleries in Japan, and she won the Japanese Nissen-bijutsu Award in 1967 and 1968.

Dom Lee received his MFA from the School of Visual Arts in New York City. He had solo exhibitions at the SVA in 1991 and 1992, and has illustrated a picture book, *Baseball Saved Us*. Mr. Lee lives in New Jersey.

Marie G. Lee is the author of the children's novels *Finding My Voice, If It Hadn't Been for Yoon Jun*, and *Saying Goodbye*. Her work for adults has appeared in many publications including the *The New York Times* and the *Kenyon Review*.

Just beneath the paper crane is **George Levenson**'s right hand. He lives with his family in Santa Cruz, California, where he uses both hands to fold cranes, make movies, and write stories. He is the director of Informed Democracy, a non-profit media production and distribution organization. *Photo credit: Steve Kurtz*

George Littlechild is a Plains Cree artist from Hobbema, Alberta, Canada. He dedicates his art entitled "Hiroshima: Her Story," used in *On the Wings of Peace*, to Sadako Sasaki and her story. "May her spirit live on in this painting." *Photo credit: Matthew Jacob*

Ana Maria Machado was born in Rio de Janeiro. She has published over eighty books for children and adults, including *Bem Do Seu Tamanho*

(*Just Your Size*). Her works for children have received all the main awards in Brazil, as well as some prizes abroad. She has served as member of IBBY committees and juries and is a children's book publisher.

Kam Mak was born in Hong Kong in 1961 and moved to Chinatown in New York City in 1971. While painting murals throughout the city, he became passionate about painting, and decided to pursue it at The School of Visual Arts. He illustrates book covers and has done one picture book, *The Moon of the Monarch Butterflies*. Mr. Mak is an instructor at the Fashion Institute of Technology.

Iri Maruki was born in 1901 in Asa, a Hiroshima Prefecture of Japan. **Toshi Maruki** was born in 1912 in Hokkaido, Japan. During World War II, upon hearing that an atomic bomb had been dropped on Hiroshima, they went, as a married couple, to care for Iri Maruki's family. While they were there, they observed scenes of incredible devastation that they would later paint. *The Hiroshima Panels* and *Minamata* are two such works. Although both have suffered from the remaining radiation they were exposed to while in Hiroshima, Toshi Maruki writes: "If we hadn't seen the corpses, we couldn't have painted the ghosts."

Milton Meltzer, biographer and historian, is the author of more than eighty books for young people and adults. He was born in Worcester, Massachusetts, and attended Columbia University. He has written or edited for newspapers, magazines, books, radio, television, and film. Mr. Meltzer received five nominations for the National Book Award as well as the Christopher, Jane Addams, Carter G. Woodson, Jefferson Cup, Washington Book Guild, Olive Branch, and Golden Kite awards. *Photo credit: Catherine Noren*

Wendell Minor's children's books have won awards such as Notable Children's Trade Books in Social Studies, ALA Booklist Children's Choices, International Reading Association Teacher's Choices, the John Burroughs List of Nature Books for Young Readers, and the John and Patricia Beatty Award by the California Library Association. Two of his titles are *The Seashore Book* and *Red Fox Running*. Mr. Minor has received over two hundred awards from every major graphics competition, including silver medals from the Society of Illustrators and the New York Art Directors Club.

Greg Mitchell is co-author of *Hiroshima in America*. He is also the former editor of *Nuclear Times* magazine, and his articles on Hiroshima have appeared in *The New York Times*, *Washington Post*, and a dozen other publications. He was awarded the Goldsmith Book Prize in 1992. *Photo credit: Fred Burrell*

Ken Mochizuki spent five years in Los Angeles, California, training as an actor and now works as editor, assistant editor, and staff writer for Asian American community newspapers in Seattle, Washington. His first picture book, *Baseball Saved Us*, received the 1993 Parents' Choice Award and the 1994 Washington Governor's Writers Award. His second book, *Heroes*, was published in the spring of 1995. *Photo credit: Steve Uyeno*

Kyoko Mori was born in Kobe, Japan, in 1957. She has lived in the Midwest since 1977 and holds a Ph.D. from the University of Wisconsin-Milwaukee. She is the author of three books: *Shizuko's Daughter*, *Fallout*, and *The Dream of Water*, and is associate professor of English and writer-in-residence at Saint Norbert College in De Pere, Wisconsin.

Junko Morimoto has written and illustrated many books for children published in America and Australia as well as throughout Europe, including *The White Crane*, *The Inch Boy*, and *Kojuro and the Bears*, which have received Highly Commended and Picture Book of the Year awards from the Children's Book Council of Australia. Two of her books were selected for the Bologna Children's Book Fair Exhibition in Italy. Ms. Morimoto lives in Northbridge, Australia.

Paul Morin, painter, sculptor, and musician, has traveled throughout the world to research the settings for his books such as *The Orphan Boy*, recipient of the Governor General's Award and an ALA Notable Book, and *The Ghost Dance*. Born in Calgary, Alberta, Canada, Mr. Morin now lives in a house at the edge of the forest in Ontario, Canada.

Walter Dean Myers was raised in Harlem by foster parents who enjoyed telling him stories. Writing has always been an important part of his life, and after forty published books, remains so. Besides the Margaret A.

Edwards lifetime achievement award in 1994, he has also won two Newbery honors and four Coretta Scott King Awards for his work. His latest books are *Glory Field* and *The Story of the Three Kingdoms*.

Keiko Narahashi was born in Tokyo and grew up in North Carolina. She currently resides in New York City. Her accomplishments so far include ten children's books (her first: *I Have a Friend*) and two children, Micah and Joy.

Rafal Olbinski was born and educated in Poland. He came to the United States in 1982 and now teaches at the School of Visual Arts in New York City. He has received more than one hundred awards for his illustrations and paintings, which include gold medals from the Society of Illustrators and the Art Directors Club of New York. His works appear regularly in *Newsweek*, *Time*, *Atlantic Monthly*, *Playboy*, and *The New York Times* among others.

Katherine Paterson is the author of eleven novels for children including two Newbery winners—*Bridge to Terabithia* and *Jacob Have I Loved*—a Newbery Honor Book, and two National Book Award winners. "My visits to Hiroshima still haunt me. How can I forget the shadows on stone which are the vaporized traces of once living persons, the devastating photographs of suffering and death, Sadako's poignant statue? For the love of the Japanese people I have known and for my belief that every human being, indeed, every living creature is precious to God, I must join my voice and life to the cry: Never again." *Photo credit: Jill Paton Walsh*

Jerry Pinkney has received awards from the New York Society of Illustrators, A.I.G.A. Book Shows, Art Directors Clubs across the country, and has won three Coretta Scott King Awards. He has also won two Caldecott Honor Book Awards, and a Golden Kite Award. One of his books was chosen a Year's Best Illustrated Book for Children by *The New York Times*. He has taught at several U.S. universities, most recently as Professor in the Art Department at the University of Buffalo.

James E. Ransome is a graduate of Pratt Institute and a winner of a Society of Illustrators Student Scholarship Competition. One of his books, *Aunt Flossie's Hats (And Crab Cakes Later)*, won a Parents' Choice Picture

Book Award and was a Notable Children's Book in the Field of Social Studies. He lives in Poughkeepsie, New York.

Painter **T. J. Reddy** has been the recipient of various grants including the North Carolina Arts Grant, has taught and exhibited throughout the southeast, and has published two volumes of poetry. He lives in Charlotte, North Carolina.

Enrique O. Sanchez grew up in Santo Domingo, Dominican Republic, where he studied fine arts. When he was twenty years old, he moved to the United States. He currently lives in Bar Harbor, Maine, and New York City. While he is primarily a fine artist, he has also illustrated several books for children such as *Abuela's Weave* and *Maria Molina and the Days of the Dead*.

Laila Shawa graduated from the Academia de Belle Arte in Rome, Italy. She has exhibited internationally, and her art has been featured in various books. One volume of her work has been published: *Laila Shawa, Works 1964-1996*. She has been a member of the Palestinian Union for Artists since 1968, and now resides in London, England.

Virginia Driving Hawk Sneve was born and raised on the Rosebud Reservation in South Dakota and is an enrolled member of the Rosebud Sioux tribe. She has published twelve children's books, five adult books, and several short stories, articles, and poems. She and her husband, Vance, have three children and four grandchildren.

Rigoberta Menchú Tum, a Guatemalan Indian-rights activist, won the 1992 Nobel Peace Prize. She is a Mayan of the Quiché group from northwestern Guatemala who gained international prominence in 1983 through her book, *I, Rigoberta Menchú*. A spokeswoman for indigenous peoples and the victims of oppression, she says: "The only thing I wish for is freedom for Indians wherever they are. As the end of the twentieth century approaches, we hope that our continent will be pluralistic."

Martin Waddell was born in 1941 in Belfast, Northern Ireland. He has published titles internationally, winning The Other Award, the Smarties

Prize, and the Sheffield Book Award for his children's books *Starry Night* and *Can't You Sleep Little Bear?*. He and his wife, Rosaleen, have three children—Thomas Mayne, David Martin, and Peter Matthew.

Yoko Kawashima Watkins's first children's book, *So Far from the Bamboo Grove*, won a Parents' Choice Award and a Judy Lopez Memorial Award, and was an NTCE Teacher's Choice Book and SLJ Best Book of the Year for 1986. Her most recent book is *My Brother, My Sister and I*. Ms. Watkins grew up in Nanam, Korea, a daughter of Japanese parents. She met her husband, Donald Watkins, at a U. S. Air Force base where she worked as a translator. The Watkins live in Brewster, Massachusetts.

Bruce Weinstock attended the Tyler School of Art and Temple University, graduating with a BFA in Illustration. He has lectured at the Parsons School of Design and the School of Visual Arts, among others. His clients include *The New York Times*, *The New York Daily News*, PC *Magazine*, and the *Chicago Tribune*.

As a teenager, **Nobuhiko Yabuki** was attracted to graphic design and was influenced by the Japanese artist Makoto Wada. Later, he focused on illustrations which expressed contemporary pop culture and landscapes. Recently, he has tried to produce pictures that have a Japanese touch, using India ink and Japanese paints. His ultimate dream is to produce illustrations that can be appreciated as a tableau.

1990 Caldecott Medalist **Ed Young** has illustrated over fifty books for children (including *Sadako*, the story of a Hiroshima girl who died of radiation sickness), five of which he has also written. He grew up in Shanghai, China, moved to Hong Kong, and came to the United States as a young man on a student visa. Mr. Young has taught at various U.S. institutes and universities, and currently lives in Hastings-on-Hudson, New York, with his wife, Filomena. *Photo credit: Sean Kernan*

✎ Bibliography of Resource Materials

HIROSHIMA/NAGASAKI and ATOMIC WAR
For Adults

Boyer, Paul. *By the Bomb's Early Light: American Thought and Culture at the Dawn of the Atomic Age* (New York: Pantheon, 1985). What the coming of the atomic bomb did to American society during the late 1940s.

Committee for the Compilation of Materials on Damage Caused by the Atomic Bombs. *Hiroshima and Nagasaki* (New York: Basic Books, 1981). The definitive text on the bomb's physical, medical, and long-term effects on its victims.

Del Tredici, Robert. *At Work in the Fields of the Bomb* (New York: Harper and Row, Perennial Library, 1987). Interviews, field notes, and photographs concerned with the production and use of nuclear arsenals.

Glasstone, Samuel, and Philip J. Dolan, eds. *Effects of Nuclear Weapons*. 3rd ed. (Washington, D.C.: United States Government Printing Office, 1983).

Hersey, John. *Hiroshima* (New York: Bantam, 1985). First published in 1946, this masterpiece of reporting explores the experiences of six survivors of the atomic attack.

Ibuse, Masuji. *Black Rain* (New York: Bantam, 1985). The classic novel about victims and survivors of Hiroshima in the immediate aftermath of the bombings.

Johnson, Katherine, with John F. Rasche. *Hiroshima: Chronicles of a Survivor* (Branden Books, 1994). Written by a former teacher at Hiroshima Girls' School, this story paints a unique picture of life in Hiroshima. Illustrated.

Lanouette, William. "Why We Dropped the Bomb." *Civilization*, The Magazine of the Library of Congress (January/February 1995), 28-39. The diplomatic and political factors that played a role in the decision to drop the bomb.

Lifton, Robert, and Greg Mitchell. *Hiroshima in America: Fifty Years of Denial* (New York: Putnam/Grosset, 1995). The recent Smithsonian incident once again exposed "America's raw nerve," sensitivity to the bombings. Lifton and Mitchell trace personal, political, cultural, and psychological responses to Hiroshima since 1945.

Rhodes, Richard. *The Making of the Atomic Bomb* (New York: Simon and Schuster, 1986). An acclaimed study of how the bomb came to be, with a focus on the physicists.

Schell, Johnathan. *The Fate of the Earth* (New York: Avon, 1982). Examines how nuclear weapons imperil all life on the planet for all time, making disarmament necessary.

Sherwin, Martin J. *A World Destroyed: Hiroshima and the Origins of the Arms Race* (New York: Vintage, 1982). How the making and use of the bomb fueled the cold war.

The Tides Foundation. *Beyond the Bomb: Dismantling Nuclear Weapons and Disposing of Their Radioactive Wastes* (San Francisco, 1994). An excellent, well-researched 26-page booklet. Explains the science and myths about disposal of 50,000 nuclear warheads. Available from Nuclear Safety Campaign, 1914 North 34th Street, Suite 407, Seattle, WA 98103.

For Children

Coerr, Eleanor. *Sadako* (New York: Putnam, 1993). The story of Sadako Sasaki, movingly depicted in Ed Young's beautiful pastel paintings. A companion to the video *Sadako and the Thousand Paper Cranes*.

———. *Sadako and the Thousand Paper Cranes* (New York: Putnam, 1977). Based on the true story of Sadako Sasaki.

Hamanaka, Sheila. *Peace Crane* (New York: Morrow Junior Books, 1995). Poem in picture book form about the eternal longing for peace by the world's children, from Sadako Sasaki to urban youth.

Japanese Broadcasting Corporation, ed. *Unforgettable Fire: Pictures Drawn by Atomic Bomb Survivors* (New York: Pantheon, 1977). Japanese survivors paint, sketch, and describe (in words) their experiences.

Lifton, Betty Jean. *A Place Called Hiroshima* (New York: Kodansha, 1985). A visit to Hiroshima four decades after the atomic bombing, with photographs by Eikoh Hosoe.

Maruki, Toshi. *Hiroshima No Pika* (New York: Lothrop, Lee and Shepard Books, 1982). Award-winning true story of a little girl named Mii who survived the bombing. Illustrated picture book by an outstanding Japanese artist.

Nagai, Dr. Takashi, compiler. *Living Beneath the Atomic Cloud: Testimonies of the Children of Nagasaki* (Wilmington, OH: Wilmington College Peace Resource Center, 1984). Personal accounts by children and youth of the bombing and its impact on them and their families. Illustrated.

Nakazawa, Keiji. *Barefoot Gen: A Cartoon Story of Hiroshima* (Project Gen, 1987; also Penguin, 1990). Powerful depiction of wartime life in Japan and the bombing, created by a survivor who was seven years old at the time. Nakazawa has dedicated his life to telling this story in several novel-length volumes. Highly recommended. Comic book format, in black and white.

———. *Barefoot Gen: The Day After* (New Society Publishers, 1989). Picks up the story the day after the bombing as Gen struggles for survival. Comic book format.

———. *Barefoot Gen: Life After the Bomb* (New Society Publishers, 1989). The series continues as Gen, his mother and baby brother search for a place to live. Comic book format.

———. *I Saw It: The Atomic Bombing of Hiroshima* (Seattle: Educomics, 1982). Nakazawa's true life story, from his earliest memories through the bombing and up to the present. Comic book format, full color. ($2 from Educomics, P.O. Box 45831 Seattle, WA 98145.)

Nasu, Masumoto. *Children of the Paper Crane* (M.E. Sharpe, 1991). Detailed story of Sadako, and her classmates who were responsible for the Children's Monument in Hiroshima's Peace Park after her death.

Audiovisuals for Adults

Bound by the Wind (VHS, 40 min.). Since 1945 more than nineteen hundred nuclear weapons have been detonated worldwide in tests above and below ground. Video studies the impact of tests on people who lived downwind from U.S., Soviet, and French test sites, and their organizing efforts.

Deadly Deception: General Electric, Nuclear Weapons & Our Environment (VHS, 30 min.). Debra Chasnoff, 1991. "Exposes the terrifying human and environmental cost of G.E.'s nuclear weapons development," and reveals secret facilities and release of toxins.

Does the United States Need Nuclear Weapons? (VHS, 28 min.). Center for Defense Information, 1994. A look at the history of atomic weapons, their buildup, and how we could actually work toward their elimination.

Hellfire: A Journey from Hiroshima (1/2" VHS, 57 min.). The Maruki Film Project, John Junkerman and John Dower, 1985. Documentary on remarkable artists Toshi and Iri Maruki, their peace efforts, and their monumental paintings on Hiroshima, the Rape of Nanking, Auschwitz, Okinawa, and their collaborative work, "Hell."

Hiroshima: The People's Legacy (1/2" VHS, 45 min.). Extremely moving look at drawings and paintings done by survivors, many of whom share their personal stories.

Lost Generation (16mm, color, 20 min.). Hiroshima/Nagasaki Pub. Co., 1982. In 1945-46 the U.S. Strategic Bombing Survey filmed thousands of feet of color film of the bombs' devastation. It was classified secret and not released until 1979. People who were in that 1945 footage now tell of their lives in the interim.

The Military and the Environment (VHS, 29 min.). Sandy Gottlieb, Center for Defense Information, 1990. Experts shed light on the extent of the military's secret and ineffective disposal of deadly nuclear waste, nerve gas, and hundreds of toxic chemicals. The Center for Defense Information was created by high-ranking former U.S. military officers.

Scrapping Nuclear Weapons (VHS, 25 min.). Center for Defense Information, 1992. The possible dismantling of thousands of nuclear bombs creates a new problem: how to dispose of their radioactive elements.

Audiovisuals for Children

How to Fold a Paper Crane (VHS, color, 30 min.). Informed Democracy, 1994. A companion to the award-winning video *Sadako and the Thousand Paper Cranes*. A whimsical pair of hands, guided by a lively narrator, demonstrates how to fold a crane. Accompanied by American sign language, the program is divided into segments to accommodate different levels of skill and speed.

On a Paper Crane: Tomoko's Adventure (VHS, color, 27 min.). Peace Anime no Kai, 1994. Touching and imaginative animated story about a sixth grader who goes to visit the Hiroshima Peace Park. Magically, Sadako's statue comes to life and tells her story.

Sadako and the Thousand Paper Cranes (VHS, color, 30 min.). Informed Democracy, 1990. Caldecott award-winning artist Ed Young created several hundred pastel paintings for this version of Sadako's story. Vividly narrated by Liv Ullman, with solo guitar soundtrack performed by George Winston. (Informed Democracy, P.O. Box 67, Santa Cruz, CA 95063.)

PEACE AND CONFLICT RESOLUTION
For Adults

Educators for Social Responsibility. *Conflict Resolution in the Middle School: A Curriculum and Teaching Guide* (1994).

————. *Elementary Perspectives I: Teaching Concepts of Peace and Conflict* (1990).

Fry-Miller, Kathleen, and Judith Myers-Walls. *Young Peacemakers Project Book* (Brethren Press, 1988). Treasure trove of imaginative learning activities for ages 3-10, suitable even for less experienced educators and caregivers. Themes are environment, understanding people, and making peace. Illustrated, large format.

Kreidler, William J. *Creative Conflict Resolution: More Than 200 Activities for Keeping Peace in the Classroom, K-6* (Scott Foresman, 1984). Extremely concrete and usable book with an appendix of worksheets and game cards.

McGinnis, Kathleen, and Barbara Oehlberg. *Starting Out Right: Nurturing Young Children as Peacemakers* (Institute for Peace and Justice, 1987). Authors are peace educators and parents who understand how violence, consumerism, racism, sexism, ageism, and nationalism undermine the struggle for peace and justice. Age-appropriate, doable plans and ideas for building peacemaking behavior in children.

Vos Wezeman, Phyllis. *Peacemaking Creatively Through the Arts* (Educational Ministries, 1990). Fresh, innovative ideas that foster global awareness, peace, and conflict resolution. Includes a full range of activities including architecture, art, writing, cooking, dance, drama, music, photography, puppetry, and storytelling. Large format.

For Children

Caduto, Michael J., and Joseph Bruchac. *Keepers of the Earth: Native American Stories and Environmental Activities for Children* (Fulcrum Inc., 1989). 21 stories, each followed by discussion guide, questions, and a couple of pages of activity suggestions for different age levels from preschool to high school. Excellent. Large format.

Carter, Jimmy. *Talking Peace* (New York: Dutton, 1993). Former president of the United States offers youthful readers his insights on resolving problems that often lead to violence.

Durell, Ann, and Marilyn Sachs, eds. *The Big Book for Peace* (New York: Dutton, 1990). Thirty best known and loved authors and illustrators celebrate the idea of living peacefully—for young children.

Moore, Joy Hofacker. *Ted Studebaker: A Man Who Loved Peace* (Herald Press, 1987). Excellent true-life story of a conscientious objector who "gave his life helping people rather than fighting them as a soldier."

Many of the resources listed above are available through the Peace Resource Center Hiroshima/Nagasaki Memorial Collection, Pyle Center, P.O. Box 1183, Wilmington College, Wilmington, Ohio 45177, (513) 382-5338. Request their excellent, annotated Peace Education Resources catalogs for books and/or audiovisual materials.

Illustration from *Sadako* by Ed Young

These Peace Organizations have been chosen to benefit from royalties from the sale of this book.

AMNESTY INTERNATIONAL USA
322 Eighth Avenue, New York, NY 10001-4808 • (212) 807-8400 • Fax: (212) 627-1451

Amnesty International is a worldwide voluntary movement that works to prevent some of the gravest violations by governments of people's fundamental human rights. The main focus of its campaigning is to: free all prisoners of conscience (men, women, and children imprisoned for their beliefs, color, ethnic origin, sex, language, or religions, provided they have neither used nor advocated violence); ensure fair and prompt trials for political prisoners; abolish the death penalty, torture, and other cruel treatment of prisoners; and end political killings and "disappearances."

FOR OUR CHILDREN'S SAKE FOUNDATION
240 Second Avenue New York, NY 10003 • (212) 868-2954 • Fax: (212) 643-1693

Our goal is to have a community-based program at a learning center in Harlem, with outreach components enabling us to bring our resources and ideas to other communities. The center will be a place where individuals, schools, and organizations can learn how to utilize the creative, expressive, and cultural arts with young people to stimulate their interest and involvement in global citizenship and peacemaking activities.

FRIENDS OF HIBAKUSHA
1759 Sutter Street San Francisco, CA 94115 • (415) 567-7599

The Friends of Hibakusha is a non-profit organization of volunteers concerned about the health and welfare of the American survivors of the Hiroshima and Nagasaki atomic bombings. We bring their message of peace to children and adults through our peace education activities. Our activities include a survivor's oral history project, participation in biennial medical visits by Japanese doctors, and community education projects.

Our mission is to provide services and assistance to U.S. hibakusha, to work for peace by educating the American public about the effects of the atomic bomb and nuclear holocaust, and to encourage research into the medical effects of radiation exposure, towards establishing medical programs in conjunction with other radiation victims (atomic vets, downwinders, uranium miners, Pacific Islanders).